3/15

Wahida Clark Presents Publishing
60 Evergreen Place
Suite 904
East Orange, New Jersey 07018
973-678-9982
www.wclarkpublishing.com
www.acreativenuance.com

Enemy Bloodline by Umar Quadeer
ISBN-13: 978-1-936649-07-5 (print)
ISBN-13: 978-1-936649-03-7 (e-book)
LCCN 2014904048

Library of Congress Cataloging-In-Publication Data:
1. Behind enemy lines 2. Mafia wars 3. Big money hustlas 4. Philly black mafia 5. Thug life 6. The streets

Cover design and layout by Nuance Art, LLC
Book design by Nuance Art, LLC
nuanceart@acreativenuance.com

For More information contact:
Sherry Porter
sherry@wclarkpublishing.com
973-678-9982

UMAR QUADEER

ACKNOWLEDGMENTS

In the name of God, the most beneficial, most merciful, and I praise and thank Him for all the blessings placed upon me.

While growing up in Philadelphia, I've met life experiences similar to some, yet perplexing to others. Putting my street life to the side and focusing on my career has put my mind in the right place. In addition, I'm motivated to inspire individuals with talent to look beyond their personal hardships and focus on striving for perfection.

Thank you, Mom, for supporting me and inspiring me to stay focused on my craft. You are the Phil Jackson of my plans. I would like to thank my father, Ruben Gober, for teaching me how to use my talents at the age of nine. I want to thank my children, Aamirah, Rafi, and Isiah, for believing in their father.

I'd like to thank my brother, Gobe-Raw, for being there for me during some of the most critical times in my life. It's GryndMode! And to Teddy and Rica, I love you guys.

To my right-hand man, Deen, thanks for supporting me through my incarceration. You don't find too many friends like you.

To my cuzzo, Bishop of Crunk, nigga, we might bump heads but you are a networking genius. Let's get this money!

To my Atlanta Muslim brothers, Omar, Hamza, and Raheem. You brothers showed me how Allah will bless you when you invest your money in something legal instead of something illegal. As-Salamulaikum!

To the mothers of my children, we share a special bond that no one can break.

What's up to Slaughter, Rock Smalls, Bloody Tribe and Homicide.

Shout outs to all the incarcerated brothers that never hated, and motivated me to build my craft. I don't know how I would've made it through my bid without my old-head, Ramzadeen. Peace!

SPECIAL REST IN PEACE DEDICATION

And to my grandmother, Mrs. Mary Gober, you are my heart, my soul, my inspiration, and the air that I breathe. You are the only woman that I've met whose spirit and character is so humble, warm, and comforting. May you rest in peace, and I love you. I'm doing this for you! Tell Grandpa that I still remember when he used to make us biscuits and coffee for breakfast.

REST IN PEACE TO ALL OF MY NORTH PHILLY FALLEN SOLDIERS:

Black Dee, Tarik, Little Derrick, Ikey, Kenny Bell, T-Ratic, Saleem, Snork, Eliot, ZonGodi, Reds, Omar, Manseeny, Skinny Bam, Starks, Roni, Lord Gore, Little Josh, Mukkah, Jig, Mark-Mark, Bradley, Little Bradley, Delaney, Grams, Little Kev, Sweet Pea and my good brother, YB from Detroit. All murdered at early ages.
Stop the Violence!

Chapter One
THE EYES OF A DEMON

"**N**iggas kidnapped my wife? I'm 'bout to murder something!" yelled Cash, a light-skinned black mob boss from North Philly.

"Whoever did this is going to pay with their life!" said Reel, who was Cash's muscle and under boss. He was a stocky gangster standing at 5-feet 11-inches and 220 pounds of solid muscle.

Cash inserted his key into the door of the BBF headquarters. The two-story brownstone stood on the corner of Twentieth and Brown on its own little hill, like royalty. He pushed open the double-doors and raced across the hardwood floor. The living room walls were painted black, and a light was always shining in through at least one of the windows. Cash was restless, so he took a seat on his red Italian leather sofa. "You goddamn right they're going to pay," he said, feeling violent.

"You sure she ain't playing a trick on you for you fucking Tanya with the fat ass?" said Reel.

"Dog, she called my phone crying, talkin' 'bout they had her in a fucking trunk! My wife don't play those type of games." Cash reached inside his pants pocket and placed a plastic sandwich bag on the coffee table. Inside the bag was a gram of cocaine. He spread the powdery, soft white substance on a dollar bill, and then sniffed a line. The rest went back inside his pocket. "Mutherfuckers going to pay!" He pulled his gun off his waist, placed it on his lap, and stared into Reel's eyes.

"Ay man, put that thing up. It's nothing but family here, bro," said Reel, feeling intimidated.

Cash ignored Reel's statement and took another sniff of cocaine until there was none left on the dollar bill.

"Take it easy with that stuff, man," said Chips, who was Capo status. He was a tall, brown-skinned, slim gangster with tattoos on his neck and face.

Cash picked up the remote control, and his eyes grew wide. "I'm going to kill somebody!" He threw the remote control at his 49-inch LCD TV that was mounted to the wall. It smashed into the TV, leaving a large crack in the screen. "Fuck it, I'll buy another one." Cash opened up a mahogany colored Cigar case from off the coffee table. "This ain't no movie, niggas!" he snapped. Cash lit up his Cuban cigar as Reel and Chips watched, wondering what was next. "I'm the real Scarface, mutherfucker!" He stared at the cloudy sky through the windows on the ceiling and blew smoke out his nose.

"Don't worry 'bout shit, big homie. We gone get her back," said Reel, trying to calm his boss down before he lost it.

Cash held back the hurt in his heart. He didn't want to seem weak in front of his crew. "Follow me." He stood and headed through the doors at the far end of the room.

"We going to get her back, boss," Chips said, staring at the portrait of Cash and his wife Porsha inside of a huge gold frame decorating the wall.

Cash walked behind the bar and placed his gun on the counter. Then he grabbed a bottle of Moet from the top shelf, popped the cork, and poured it into a crystal flute.

Champagne raced to the top of the glass while the bubbles slowly followed.

"Here you go, Reel," said Cash, handing Reel his drink.

Cash poured Chips and himself a glass of champagne and felt a part of his soul missing. But even though he loved his wife, he loved the streets more. A thousand thoughts raced through his mind.

The ringing cell phone broke the silence. He looked at the private number and hesitated to answer. ". . . Hello?"

"You got one hour to deliver five hundred thousand dollars to 3967 Myrtlewood Street, or your bitch is dead," said the kidnapper. "Put the money in the trashcan in front of the address I gave you."

Dial tone.

Cash shook his head in disbelief. "This can't be happening!" he said with anger.

"Who was that?" Reel asked.

"They said they want the money in an hour or sh. Sh. She's dead," said Cash.

"Cash, just pay them the money," said Reel. "We a hit the street and make it back, man. Think about your wife."

"Do you really think they gone give me my wife back? No! She's done! It's over, but I'll tell you this: whoever did this I'm a kill they whole family starting with the children!" Cash promised. "I know them bastards going to kill her!" he yelled. "I can't show my enemies no weakness. If I let her die, niggas going to know that I'm heartless."

"Cash, this is Porsha we talking about. She been holding you down since day one," said Reel.

"In this game you got to be able to grow numb to love, because if not, these streets a eat you alive!" Cash swigged his drink.

"You mean to tell me you got the money, but you not going to pay your wife's ransom because you don't want to look soft in the street?" Reel asked.

"That's exactly what I'm saying."

"That's fucked, Cash!"

"Life is fucked up, Reel," said Cash.

Reel shook his head in disbelief.

Cash was dying inside about the kidnapping. He couldn't wait to get revenge on all his enemies, and he daydreamed of killing whoever was responsible. Images of his wife flashed in his mind. He opened up a drawer behind the bar and pulled out seven grams of cocaine. "I'm 'bout to get fucked up," he said, turning toward Reel, who was now pointing a 9-millimeter Kel-Tec pistol in his face.

"What the fu—" asked Cash.

"Don't move! You reach for your gun, and I'll blow your fucking head off!"

"Get that gun out my face!" Cash peeked at his Uzi pro lying on the table. "Fuck you!" he yelled, reaching for his gun.

With perfect timing, Chips swung a straight jab that landed on Cash's jaw. The impact of the hard punch sent him to his knees.

Chips picked up Cash's gun from off the counter.

"Didn't I tell you don't move?" Reel aimed his pistol at Cash's head, ready to pull the trigger.

"Reel, what the fuck is you doing?" Cash asked curiously, while stumbling back to his feet holding his jaw.

Reel snapped, "You know exactly what this is about! You not breaking us off a piece of the American pie."

"Man, fuck you!" Cash charged at Reel with rage.

Reel's gun went off, sending two hot slugs in Cash's right and left kneecap.

Cash fell to the ground. "You bitch muthafucka! You hating ass nigga!" said Cash, feeling the horrible pain. "Kill me then, muthafucka!" he said as blood soaked the carpet.

"Now, where is the big safe that you got here?" asked Reel.

"Man, I'm not telling you shit!" Cash winced.

"Oh, you think this is a game?" Chips walked to the bar and grabbed a bottle of 360 Vodka and popped the top off. He stood over Cash, then poured vodka on his bullet wounds.

"Ah!" yelled Cash, leaping up on one leg. He tried to tackle Chips. "Im a kill y'all!"

Chips kicked Cash in the face. "Uhgh!"

Cash fell flat on his stomach. "You mutherfuckas is dead!" he said, coughing blood.

"Tell us where the safe at, or I'm a fuck you up real bad," said Chips.

"If you don't get your little bitch ass outta here. You think Reel cares about you? He going to do your ass the same way as soon as you make one mistake," said Cash, trying to talk some sense into Chips.

Reel disagreed. "Shut the fuck up, Cash! I have been carrying the Black Boss Family on my shoulders for five years! You don't do shit but get paid!"

Cash tried to hide his fear. All the years that he terrorized the streets, he never knew it would end up like this. He started to regret ever trusting them. All the arguments and fights between them were now crawling from under the rug. "Okay, you win. Just take the money. That's what you want, Reel?"

"Where is the damn safe?" Chips yelled, beating Cash's kneecaps with the empty vodka bottle.

"Ah! Okay, okay. It's behind the portrait of me and my wife!" Cash said. "I hope y'all niggas burn in hell."

Chips ran to the painting and pushed it off the wall, revealing a huge safe.

Reel kicked Cash hard in the ribs. "What's the combo!" he demanded.

"Okay, bro, you got it. It's 23-65-56."

Chips tried the combination. "It's not working!" he said, trying once more.

"You playing games with us, Cash?" asked Reel.

"No, nigga, I just told you the combo!" he said, hoping for no more punishment.

"I'm a try one more time, and if this shit don't work, I'm a stab this nigga in his kneecaps," said Chips.

"You got to turn right, left, then right," said Cash.

Chips followed directions. A few quick turns of the dial and the safe was open.

Reel and Chips' eyes began to glow after seeing the safe filled with huge piles of one hundred dollar bills stacked neatly.

"Go get some bags!" Reel said, scanning the room.

Chips ran to the kitchen and slammed open drawers and cabinets. "Got it!" he yelled, noticing the box of Glad 50-gallon bags under the sink. He raced back to the safe and began sweeping the money into the trash bags.

Cash tried to negotiate for his life. "Reel, let's be reasonable, man. You take the money and leave and I'll let bygones be bygones."

"Oh really? So you can come back for me? Where's the kilos you copped off Cannon?"

Cash played stupid. "All the keys I got is on the streets."

"I don't believe you! You lying piece of shit. You got one more chance to tell me where the coke at, or I'm a cut your fuckin' legs off while you still breathing!"

Cash heard the sound of Reel's 9-millimeter cocking back. "Okay! Okay! I'll tell you," Cash exclaimed as he pointed to the ceiling.

"Go get that shit, Chips!" said Reel.

Chips grabbed a chair and stood on it. He reached and pushed the panel to the side. Then he pulled on the handle of the bag, and it fell to the floor causing a loud thump.

"Open it!" Reel demanded.

Chips snatched the bag open. "Damn! This shit is loaded!"

Reel held the gun at Cash's head with an angry look on his face. "Damn, Mr. Untouchable, you have been holding out on us. I guess what they say is true. Stingy niggas be the rich ones." Reel felt guilty about killing Cash because the two grew up together.

Cash clasped his hands in prayer. "Lord, please don't let this happen." Then he prayed silently and closed his eyes.

Seconds later, he opened his eyes to his attacker. "Please, Reel, don't kill me, dog. Don't kill me. Please!" he begged for mercy.

"That's right. Pray, nigga. 'Cause you gone need a prayer where you going," Reel snapped, aiming his gun at Cash's head.

Reel wanted to be the next king of the BBF. With Cash out the way, he would be next up to control the streets.

"Do what you got to do, nigga," said Cash as tears fell down his cheeks.

"Oh, I am. You should have paid the money, dick head. Now I got to kill your wife too," Reel said cold-heartedly.

"You bastard! You slimy muthafucka!" Cash cried.

Reel aimed his weapon against his head. "I didn't know you would be my fifth murder seal. You remember my third murder seal, right? How can you forget that? You the one put it on there."

Cash remembered the day when Reel killed one of his best friends over a drug corner. Later on that night, Cash gave Reel his murder seal by pressing a hot ice pick into Reel's chest and across his skin, a BBF tradition.

Cash snapped back into reality. "Far as we go back, you gone do me like this, nigga?"

"That was then and this now," said Reel, aiming his gun at Cash's forehead.

Blouww!

Blood sprayed the carpet. "I bet you don't remember nothing now." Reel watched Cash die slow, gasping for air. He shot two more times, stopping his body from trembling. "Come on, Chips! Let's get the fuck out of here!"

Chapter Two
YOUNG BOSS

Sixteen-year-old Giovanni Henchmen saw and heard some things that he shouldn't have after opening his blinds and his bedroom window.

"Yeah, girl. I'm telling you that my boo, Chips, buys me whatever I want. He's going to be the next king of the Black Boss Family. That nigga Reel don't do nothing but sit on his lazy ass," said the dark-skinned dime piece named Cola. She sat on the stoop braiding her best friend Princess' hair.

"He told you that, girl?" said Princess with a smile, exposing her dimples.

"What do you mean did he tell me that? You fake Lauren-London-looking bitch," she joked.

"Fuck you!" said Princess.

"Of course, he tells me everything. He's just using Reel for his connect. He's going to be the next king, and that means more money for me." Cola laughed.

"Them bitches always running they mouth," Giovanni complained, walking his nearly six-foot-tall frame downstairs into the living room. "Buy her everything she want? How am I supposed to compete to get a girl like that?" he asked aloud.

Spaz pushed the power button on the TV, and the morning news caught his attention.

"Andrew Smith was found dead inside of his home this afternoon. His wife, Porsha Smith, was found just blocks away inside of a trunk of a car. Mrs. Smith was subpoenaed to testify against a member of The Black Boss Family in a court hearing on the third of January. Federal agents believe that could have been the motive for her death. Agents did a gang sweep on the BBF members. The raids began before dawn, and when they ended, street bosses, underbosses, foot soldiers, and associates from all over the city were caught up in a sweep that involved more than one hundred law enforcement officers," the reporter announced.

The TV flashed to a press conference. Federal Agent Mark Rizzo was a thirty-five-year-old short, dark haired, fair-skinned man of Italian descent. He began to speak. "We are determined to eradicate these criminal enterprises once and for all and bring all of them to justice."

The TV flashed back to the newscaster. "Members of the Black Boss Family were charged with sixteen separate indictments. They took a big hit earlier today. The charges stemmed from murder, gambling, loan sharking, arson, extortion, drug trafficking, robbery, and racketeering. Some of these allegations involve classic mob hits to eliminate rivals. Nineteen-year-old Todd Smith was brutally gunned down for stepping on one of the BBF member's shoes at a movie theater on Broad and Cecil B. Moor. We will keep you posted as the trials move forward. This is Mike Arnold, reporting live from City Hall," said the newscaster with a fake smile.

If that was me, I would have never got caught. Giovanni was used to seeing ballers from the BBF with all the women, money, cars and clothes. *I want to get money like that. What if I was that rich?* He cut the TV off and walked into the bathroom to wash up. Giovanni brushed his low cut hair as a roach climbed across the mirror, obscuring a complete view of his light green eyes and handsome face. He plucked the roach to the floor, and then stepped on it. "I hate these motherfuckin' roaches!" The roach infestations weren't the only things he hated in the house. Spaz also hated the fact that he couldn't walk barefoot in his living room because the old damaged wooden floor put splinters in the bottom of his feet. Many nights he recalled taking cold showers because of the gas being cut off, and his mother had to use the next door neighbor's electricity by connecting a long extension cord from their house to hers. No matter how many times he sprayed roaches with Raid, the bugs would multiply and come back to crawl on the walls, floors, and counters. He shook his head with repugnance. *One day, I'm a buy my mom a house so she will never have to pay rent!* He put on his backpack and headed out into the treacherous North Philadelphia streets. He slammed the front door on his way outside.

"Stop slamming my damn door!" his mother screamed with her head sticking out of her bedroom window. "And make sure you come straight home from school, boy!" Pearl said.

"All right, Mom!" he said with an attitude.

"I'm not playing with you, boy. I'm tired of you getting in trouble on the streets," she said, referring to the incident where Giovanni and two of his friends got arrested for driving a stolen car. He swore up and down that he didn't know the car was stolen, but she didn't believe him. Pearl knew she had to keep her eyes on him because he was turning out to be just like his father. Nevertheless, she couldn't help but admire her son walking up the street like a growing lion in the jungle. "What time are you coming home, young man?"

"I'll be home after school, Mom. Stop sweating me!" said Giovanni.

Growing up in the ghetto around young thugs gave Giovanni hood swag. His father nicknamed him Spaz, stemming from the temper tantrums he used to throw as a child. The hood kept that name alive.

Pearl rolled her eyes instead of responding to her son's smart mouth. Spaz's mother was an Italian beauty queen named Pearl Gravamina. She moved to Philadelphia after being ostracized by her Italian family for getting pregnant by a black man. "Either you get an abortion, or you get out of my house!" were the words from her mother. Pearl chose to keep her baby and moved to Philly with the child's father, Saleem Henchmen aka Flash.

Saleem got the nickname Flash because of his flashy lifestyle. He wore top designer clothes, jewelry, and drove fancy cars. Ten years after Spaz was born, Flash was arrested and sentenced to ten years in prison. During Flash's absence, Pearl utilized her time with too much partying and drugs. As the years crept by, depression burned her mind, body, and soul to the ground. Pearl was known as old baggage.

Spaz began walking up the street on his way to school, seeing piles of trash in front of his neighbors' doors. Graffiti decorated the walls, and empty crack bags could be seen everywhere. Spaz daydreamed of the day he could buy a mansion; that was his fantasy.

Stuck in his future thoughts, he crossed the street and a Benz SUV sitting on 26-inch rims raced toward him. His life flashed before his eyes as the Benz skidded to a complete stop, inches from hitting him.

Reel jumped out of the Benz in a rage. "Are you crazy? I almost hit your little ass!"

Still in shock, Spaz was speechless and out of breath.

Reel's rage started to cool. "Don't I know you from somewhere, young buck?"

Spaz finally spoke. "Uh, I live across the street."

"Oh yeah, that's right. You're Pearl's son." Reel smiled. "Come on, young buck. Get in, so I can take you to school."

"I . . . I don't know if that's a good idea."

Reel laughed as he mocked Spaz. "You, you don't know if that's a good idea? Man, get in the car." Reel climbed into the driver's side while Spaz hesitated. "Come on, man, I don't have all day."

Spaz found his courage to get into the car.

Reel cruised through the streets of North Philly until they arrived at Ben Franklin High School. The block was crowded with teenagers laughing and talking to one another while walking toward the entrance.

The security guards at the top of the stairway yelled to students, "Two straight lines. Females on the left and males on the right."

Reel parked and started schooling Spaz about the importance of a good education. After the lecture he reached in his pocket, grabbed a roll of money, and peeled off a fifty-dollar bill. "Here. Take this, young buck. That should hold you down for a minute. Now go ahead and handle your business before you're late."

Spaz looked at the bill and smiled. "Good looking out, Reel."

"Aw, man, it's nothing. Just tell your mom that Big Reel said what's up?"

Spaz took the money and stepped out the car. "Okay, I got you." He admired Reel as he sped off and up the block in his fancy car.

"Ayo, Spaz. Come over here, nigga!" Grams said from across the street after he and Slugger watched Spaz hop out of Reel's Benz. Grams and Slugger were Spaz's best friends, and they had earned a reputation for robbing pizza delivery trucks for a quick dollar.

"What's up, gang?" Spaz said, jogging over to where they stood. He shook their hands, out of breath. "What's good?"

"What you doing in a car with Reel?" said Grams.

"How da fuck you know Reel?" Spaz asked.

"Who doesn't know him? That nigga is the new leader of the Black Boss Family. All them niggas just got locked up. He the new boss now."

"Damn, I was watching that shit on the news. But I never knew Reel was the new boss."

"Yeah, stupid. That muthafucka is rich. And if you cross him, he get you bodied. He run shit. You didn't know?"

"He said he knew my mom," said Spaz.

"That's going to be your new daddy," said Grams.

"What—nigga? You better watch your mouth," Spaz replied, throwing a few jabs at Grams.

"I was just fuckin' with you," Grams said, dodging Spaz's punches.

Slugger broke up the excitement. "Chill. Grams, cut it out, nigga! On some real shit though, we need to fuck with Reel. He a put us on paper! I been robbing since the age of thirteen, my nigga. We need to be pushing fancy cars and all that. To my mother I'm just another bill. She told me if I don't help her with the rent, she's going to kick my ass out."

"Yeah nigga, and if his mom kick him out the house, I won't have nowhere to go when I cut school. So fuck it, let's ball out."

Spaz shook his head. "That's the only reason you trying to get money is to cut school and fuck bitches over this nigga crib? You got the game fucked up. I'm trying to buy a mansion, nigga. Nice, big, swimming pool, basketball court, trips to Vegas, living the life. Y'all got me fucked up. My house looks like shit! It's roaches everywhere. And I'm tired of my mom. All she ever does is drink, smoke, and fuck niggas for a couple dollars." Spaz' words were interrupted by the school bell.

"Come on, we might as well get these classes over with," said Slugger, leading the way toward the school entrance.

"When I make my first thousand dollars, I'm dropping out," Grams said, following Slugger across the street.

"Reel gone help us make so much money that we'll be able to afford to drop out." Spaz laughed.

Spaz, Grams, and Slugger stood on the corner watching the local drug dealers make money. Reel's drug corner was like a fast food restaurant. Fiends were placing their orders to go. Hustlers served long lines of crack heads that smelled bad, looked horrible, but always managed to have money to buy drugs. They would do anything for a hit of the crack rock.

"You niggas want to know what the most valuable resource in the world is?" asked Spaz.

"Money, of course," answered Slugger.

"You wrong," said Spaz.

"Pussy," Grams said with confidence.

"You wrong too, nigga."

"Here you go with these philosophies," said Grams. "What is it then?"

"The most powerful resource on the planet is information." Spaz smiled.

"Information? This nigga crazy," said Grams.

"Information is the key. Man, it's niggas out here making a million dollars a year. How did they do it? I bet they have a formula and can teach you how to make a million. I want to know how to do everything."

"Man, I am sick and tired of wearing these same pair of Nikes. I need a new pair," Slugger complained.

Grams nodded. "I know, man. I want Stephanie's phone number, but she only goes out with the big-time hustlers."

Spaz said. "There go Reel right there."

Reel pulled up and hopped out his car with a bottle of champagne.

"Hey, y'all motherfuckers get back to work. This is not a hangout. It's a place of business!" Reel yelled to his dealers.

Spaz and his crew walked past Reel and made gestures to get his attention. As they approached Reel, his eyes lit up after seeing Spaz. Reel immediately thought of Pearl, Spaz's mother.

Pearl was extremely pretty, Italian with a black girl's body, and had the sex drive of a porno star, but after Spaz's father went to jail for ten years, she grew depressed, calling on drugs and alcohol to be her counselor. Because of their past relationship, Reel would give her money from time to time. He wondered if Spaz could possibly be his son.

"Naaaah," he mumbled. "Hey, young buck. Come here."

"What's up, Reel?" asked Spaz.

Reel stared at Spaz, observing his features. *He doesn't look nothing like me.* He reached in his pocket to give Spaz some more money. "Here, take this. Don't spend it all in one place, little man."

"Good looking, but I need to tell you something." Spaz stuffed the money in his pocket.

Reel grew concerned as he pulled Spaz to the side of the building. "Make this quick. I'm in a rush. I don't even like coming out here on this hot ass block."

Spaz looked around nervously as Chips pulled up in his Lexus. "Reel, you know we all look at you like a big brother. I want you to know you should pay close attention to the niggas in your circle. You didn't hear this from me, but Chips be running his mouth about how he does all the work, and you do nothing but sit on your ass and collect money."

Reel couldn't believe his ears as he watched Chips and Maine walk into the building.

Maine glanced at Spaz and Reel.

"BBF, nigga, that's what's up!" Reel took a deep breath and focused his attention back on Spaz. "So what the fuck you assuming, young buck?"

My mom told me to never tell my business to lil kids and females, because they will run they mouth. She should have told Chips because bad news travels fast. He fuck with my next door neighbor, and I heard her conversation about you and Chips."

"What she say?"

"She said Chips is just using you for your coke plug. That's why you need to put me and my boys down with you."

"How the fuck you know he using me for my connection? You think I'm a listen to some bitch about my homie?" Reel laughed.

"Because the streets talk. But don't worry about nothing. I got your back." Spaz lifted his shirt slightly, exposing the gun handle on his waist.

"Lil nigga, you strapped? What you know about guns?"

"I might be young, but I'm smart. Me, Grams, and Slugger already be doing stickups and stealing cars." Spaz pointed to his friends. "Grams is the dark-skinned cat over there with the scar on his face. He keeps a rusty .38 snub with him at all times. He's the quiet but deadly type. He's going to catch a body sooner or later. But he loves me to death and will never turn his back on me. My other friend is the brown-skinned, chubby nigga standing by him. That's my man Slugger. He's a straight hustler for real. I tell you no lie. He sits in the lunchroom everyday hustling nickel-bags of weed."

Reel smiled with greed. "Yeah, how old are y'all lil niggas?"

"Me and Slugger is sixteen, and Grams is seventeen."

Reel took another glance at Grams leaning up against the wall with his hand close to his gun. "Okay, you told me about your squad, but what about you? What do you have to offer?"

Spaz looked Reel in the eyes. "I'm a mastermind. I see into the future, and I see myself in a mansion, real soon."

Reel began to laugh. "You niggas is young but deadly. I don't know though. I don't think you niggas is ready."

"Man, you got us fucked up."

"Oh, I got y'all fucked up? Okay, tough guy. We gone see where your heart at. Meet me this Thursday at 11:00 p.m. sharp at the 840 Lounge."

"We will be there," said Spaz, willing to do whatever for money and power.

Chapter Three
BLOODY FINISH LINE

"**L**et's get this fucking money!" said Spaz as the three young thugs took deep, anxious breaths and turned the corner. The sky was pitch black and darkness covered the city.

Reel was sitting in front of the 840 Lounge sipping on a bottle of Dom Pérignon, surrounded by twenty-five members of the Black Boss Family. They were huddled up like a football team during an intense time out. He gazed in the distance and spotted Spaz, Grams, and Slugger walking toward them.

Spaz took a deep breath as they approached Reel.

"What's up, young bucks?" Reel said, greeting his new recruits. They returned the greeting with a head nod. "Listen up, motherfuckers. We got a fucking problem on our hands! Our problem's name is L-Rock. This motherfucker keep coming around here robbing my workers."

"I know him," Spaz said. "He goes to my school. He hangs around Sybert Street." Spaz took a sip of Dom Pérignon that Reel passed to him. He looked Reel in the eyes. "Fuck L-Rock, our loyalty is with you."

Grams held his hand by his gun and nodded in agreement.

Chips was offended. "Reel, who the fuck is these little niggas?"

Reel smiled. "Are you sure you want to know who they are? Depending on your luck, these might be the little niggas taking your place."

Chips swallowed his spit as Reel began to speak to Spaz. "Spaz, if you can handle this problem, you got a ticket into my kingdom. So this is what your lil crew needs to do . . ."

"Okay, listen. We need to handle our business. Grams, Slugger, y'all ready?" said Spaz while sitting on the steps of an abandoned house.

"Let's do it," Grams said, slipping on his leather gloves.

"You ready, Slugger?" asked Spaz.

"Hell yeah," Slugger said, pulling out a small piece of a spark plug.

"Let's go!" Spaz yelled.

"Okay, okay." Slugger and Spaz crossed the street looking both ways, tiptoeing to a dark colored Cadillac. Slugger hesitated, then threw the spark plug at the driver side window. The glass shattered. The alarm began ringing loudly.

"Oh shit!" Slugger said as he and Spaz ran for cover inside a nearby alley.

Grams pulled out a screw driver and towel and ran toward the Cadillac. He cleared the broken glass with the towel and climbed inside. Grams was nervous from the alarm ringing. "Shit!" he shouted, breaking the steering column with the screw driver.

A few minutes later, an older man opened his front door and ran into the street dressed in his underwear.

Grams cranked the ignition and pressed his foot on the gas.

"Come on, boy. I got something for your bad ass!" the elderly man shouted, aiming his shotgun at the back of his car. "Black so'm of a bitch!" he said, firing shots at Grams sitting behind the steering wheel.

"Oh shit!" Grams said, observing the front windshield shatter after the first pierced the back window.

The old man watched as his Cadillac sped up the street and bent the corner on screeching tires.

"Fuck the Black Boss Family! I ain't scared of them niggas. I'm L-Rock," the young hoodlum said. His reputation in the street made him feel like a super-thug. L-Rock's pockets were full of money, and he had a brown-skinned dime piece with light brown eyes and long curly hair as his main squeeze. The two fell in love after meeting at Big Momma's candy store last year.

"Hey sexy," L-Rock said to the young tender roni as the two hugged in the hallway.

"Hey, boo," she replied with a huge smirk.

"You ready to get up out of here?" said L-Rock.

"Yes, I'm so hungry I can eat a horse," said Moesha.

"I don't know about a horse, but I got something else you can eat."

"Shut up, nasty." Moesha shoved L-Rock on the shoulder.

"I'm just playing. Come on, baby. We going to go get some pizza. You want some pizza?"

"Are you kidding me? I'm starving. Pizza would be lovely right now."

The school bell sounded, and the students raced out the doors to their destinations. Moesha walked down the hall and out the door with her teenage lover. The couple turned the corner of Sixteenth Street and walked toward L-Rock's car.

"I'm a beat that pussy up when we get to the crib," L-Rock whispered to Moesha as he squeezed her butt.

"Whatever, nigga! You're not beating nothing." She blushed.

He escorted Moesha to the passenger side of his Crown-Vic sitting on 22-inch rims. L-Rock walked around to the driver side like he was the thugged out young prince of North Philly and well on his way to becoming king. That invincible feeling was cut short when a black Cadillac pulled up on the side of him.

Spaz and Grams exited the car wearing black hoods and Halloween masks and holding 12 gauge shotguns. Grams kept his eyes on Moesha, who was sitting on the passenger side while Spaz approached L-Rock. Spaz never felt this nervous in his life.

Slugger had the car in drive, his hand on the gear shift, and his foot on the brake.

L-Rock walked to the driver's side and as he grabbed the door handle he noticed a masked gunman approaching him.

Spaz aimed his gun at L-Rock's chest. "What's up now, motherfucker?"

Blouw!

The bullets knocked L-Rock off of his feet. He hit the ground hard with blood pouring from his midsection. He groaned from witnessing his life leave his body.

Grams sprinted towards L-Rock holding his 12 gauge. "Tell God I said what's up." He pumped three more buckshots into L-Rock's chest and face.

Moesha witnessed the murder from the passenger side and began to shriek. Cries and screams from onlookers blended in with the sounds of gunfire. L-Rock brains squirmed on the concrete. Moesha peeked out of the window, holding back her screams

Spaz aimed his gun inside L-Rocks car ready to pull the trigger and send Moesha to hell. Thoughts of killing her raced through his mind as they stared into each other's eyes. *Something is telling me not to kill you, bitch!*

Moesha closed her eyes and prayed silently. *Please God, don't let them kill me.*

"Kill that bitch!" said Grams, aiming his gun at Moesha.

"No! No! Let her live, let's go!" Spaz demanded. He shoved Grams in his back, and they jumped into the car. Slugger dropped his foot on the accelerator just as sirens sounded off nearby.

Chapter Four
TRADITIONAL SACRIFICE

"**Y**'all ready for this shit?" Reel asked as he walked into the basement followed by his BBF goons.

"Hell yeah!" one of them said. "I was born ready for BBF."

They all passed by the 70-inch plasma television mounted to a wall that had replaced the portrait of Cash and his wife Porsha and stood in a circle. Chips pulled out a sharp ice pick, flicked his lighter, and moved the flame to the tip of the blade. He held it there until the tip got scorching hot.

Reel lifted his shirt all the way to his neck, exposing his big muscular chest. He stared at Spaz.

"You know what this is, young buck?"

Spaz observed the five long slashes but couldn't find the answer.

Grams raised his hand. "I know what they represent."

Reel smiled. "You goddamn right! This is my body count. This is what separates the men from the boys." He pushed his shirt back down to his waist. "Y'all look like some lil hustling muhfuckas. But just remember, loyalty will get you rich and snitching will get you killed."

Spaz watched Chips' blade as it turned fiery red at the tip.

"You ready for your murder seal?" said Reel.

Grams took his shirt off and sat on the couch. "Let's get it!"

Reel grabbed the hot blade from Chips, who held Grams down. Then Reel pressed the hot ice pick against his skin, creating a long, blistery slash on his chest. Grams screamed and expressed his pain. "Damn that shit is hot!" He rose to his feet with a look of aggression.

Both Grams and Spaz had earned their stripes.

Spaz took his shirt off and took a seat. Reel branded the BBF murder seal on Spaz's flesh. He felt the hot blade tear through his skin, and his eyes watered from the sharp pain. "Fuck!" Spaz yelled.

Reel and Chips started to laugh. "You okay, little nigga?" asked Chips.

Slugger didn't pull the trigger, so he couldn't get a murder seal. By the pained looks that Grams and Spaz gave, he was happy that he hadn't.

Reel paced the floor. "Okay, little niggas, listen up. It's mandatory that I teach y'all the history of the BBF. Before we was the BBF, we used to be called the Rebels, a gang made up to fight police brutality. On February 29, 1996, the FBI gunned down twenty-three members of the Rebels. Our neighborhood was bombed and the rest were arrested. The offspring of the Rebels, Cool Shawn and Big-O formed the Black Boss Family. In 2010, when Cool Shawn and Big-O went to prison, Corey Blade was made boss. There were many notorious leaders in the BBF, but none like Cory Blade. His millionaire mind and drug wars spread throughout the city of Philadelphia, making the BBF the richest and bloodiest crime syndicate in US history!" Reel said. "Blade was killed in a shootout with the police, and the crown was passed to Cash." *I got him out the way. Now I'm boss.* "Cash was killed a few months ago. Now I'm the head of the BBF, and we gone ride till the casket drop, you hear me? Now y'all niggas remember this history I just gave y'all because every BBF member knows it by heart." Reel stared at his new members. "I got something for y'all." Reel gave each of them small gift wrapped boxes.

"You giving out gifts and all that?" asked Chips.

"Listen to yourself, Chips, crying over a gift. Sometimes I wonder why you are still on my team." Reel walked into a separate entrance toward his office as Chips followed. "I'm a talk to y'all in a minute," he yelled. Reel strolled inside a huge office.

"Oh, yeah, I forgot to tell you that I am having a painter come by and change the color of the rooms. Let me ask you something, Chips. Are you happy with your position?" he asked, lighting up a cigarette.

"Of course, Reel. Why wouldn't I be?"

"I heard you cut a side deal with the plug," Reel said, referring to his South Philly cocaine connection kingpin, Chris Cannon.

"He is lying!"

Reel plucked ashes in the ashtray and sat in his chair. He pulled out a 9-millimeter and aimed the barrel at Chips. "Have a seat," he said in a calm voice.

Chips regretted not having his gun on him, and remembered the moment when Reel asked him to leave it in the car. He hesitated but took a seat. "Why would I do that? I'm loyal to you." Even though Chips was scared, he remained calm.

"Unfortunately, this is not my only issue with you. In the last few weeks I heard a lot of other bad news about you," said Reel.

"I hope it's some money in this muthafucka," said Spaz, staring at his gift wrapped black box with burning curiosity. He opened his box first while Grams and Slugger watched. "Daaaamn!" Spaz said, pulling out a Ruger P90 and inspecting it like treasure.

Frantic to see if his box contained the same thing, Grams ripped his box open and pulled out his new weapon. "Hell yeah!" Grams felt like the most powerful kid in the ghetto, staring at his 40 Cal.

Slugger smiled when he saw a .45 automatic in his box. "It's on!"

"Yo, it's a letter here. Let me read this," Spaz said.

Yo, you said you and your boys is about that life. This is your final test. I want y'all to come in here and rock this nigga to sleep!

Spaz stared at the closed door where his biggest challenge awaited him. He exposed an evil grin. "Let's fuck this nigga up."

"Reel, you put me on my feet, baby. You gave me my first key. I think people are just trying to split us up because we are locking the city down. Don't feed into that bullshit." Chips tried to keep a straight face as he lied. The room grew silent. Chips glanced at the plastic on the floor, and then at the condition of the walls. None of the walls needed painting.

Oh shit!

The door flew open and Chips looked death in the eyes and witnessed Spaz, Slugger, and Grams aiming guns at him.

"What the fuck!" Chips said.

Loud whistles from Spaz and Grams' silencers opened bloody holes inside Chips' chest. Chips felt the hot slugs melting into his flesh and bones. He used his arms for a shield and fell. His bloody hands shook simultaneously.

He managed to get a few words out, while coughing blood. "You really gone do me like this, Reel?"

Reel hated to have to put his old friend to rest, but he knew it was necessary.

Slugger walked over to Chips and aimed his .45 automatic at his head.

Spaz yelled with one finger in Slugger's face. "You pop him! Nigga, we not going to be the only ones catching wreck. Shoot him in the head!"

Slugger's hand shook apprehensively as he squeezed the trigger, sending two slugs inside Chips' head.

Reel slapped Slugger on the back. "That piece of shit was a snake! That is what happens to a snake in my organization." Reel bent down and grabbed a Gucci gym bag. "I like how you handled that, Spaz. Here, take this," said Reel, throwing the gym bag that landed in Spaz's hands. "This is twenty grand worth of bundles of crack. The strip on Twenty-Fifth Street used to be Chips; now it's yours. Take Slugger and Grams down there and get money. Stack paper and don't take any shorts. Anybody got a problem, tell them you work for me."

Spaz looked at the gym bag with excitement. He finally had his chance to shine, and he loved it. "How much of this do we get to keep?"

Reel smiled. "All of it! By the time you finish with this package, you should have enough money to go into business for yourself. Here, take this number. That's my young boy. His name is Maine. There is plenty more where that came from. Tell him I sent you. He will teach y'all the ropes about hustling. Now take this bag and go get some fucking money. I got a mess to clean." Reel stared at Chips' dead body.

The next day on the south side of Philadelphia, Spaz stood on the corner shaking a pair of dice in his hand, plotting to relieve some fools of their hard earned money amongst other diabolical BBF tasks.

"Man, shoot the dice so I can get paid," said a gambler named Pooch.

Spaz shook the dice. "Come on eight. Momma need some new shoes," said Spaz, and then he rolled the dice. They bounced up against the wall and returned in front of him. "Eight, muthafuckas!" he yelled. Happy cheers came from the gamblers who won and disappointed reactions showed on the faces of the losers.

Spaz heard his ringtone and looked down at his text from Reel. It read:

Red shirt 187.

Immediately, Spaz stared at the gambler with the red sweatshirt. "Your shot, homie. I bet you crap out," said Spaz, handing him the dice.

"You got me fucked up. Bet a fifty I don't," said Pooch.

"Bet a hun'ed, nigga."

"That's a bet." Pooch dropped a hundred dollars on the ground and started shaking the dice.

Spaz watched him as he blew into the dice. "Shoot the dice, nigga," said Spaz.

Pooch bent over to throw the dice. Spaz placed the barrel of a Glock to the back of Pooch's head.

"Buck! Buck!"

Reel drove his Benz up Ridge Avenue. Maine sat on the passenger side. He looked down at his phone. He had a text from Spaz that read: *Red shirt done deal!*

Chapter Five
BLOOD CURRENCY

"**M**om?" Spaz walked inside of his mother's house calling her name. When he didn't get a response he walked up to her bedroom. "Mom!" he yelled for the fourth time, arriving at her bedroom door.

"What? Leave me alone!" Pearl said, lying comfortably on her queen-sized bed.

Spaz knocked on the door and invited himself in.

"What I tell you about barging in my room, boy?" she said, bundled up under the blanket.

"Did you know it was a thousand dollars in that old sofa downstairs?" he asked with surprise in his voice.

"What!" She threw the blanket off her.

"Yeah, I just found it," he said, handing her the money.

"Let me see this, boy," she said, making sure the money was real. She frowned as she noticed red stains on some of the bills. "This money got blood on it, Spaz. Look." She pushed a few Benjamins toward him.

"Let me see," said Spaz, observing the money. *Damn! I thought I put that aside. Wrong damn stack.* "It was so far down in the couch that I cut my hand on them raggedy springs when I realized what it was. It's not even on all the bills. See?" Spaz showed her a few of the clean bills. "You want me to wash the rest of them off though?"

Pearl inspected the other bills. " . . . Yeah, you're right. Go 'head and wash them off for me. I can't believe you even found this? God must have heard my prayers. Thank you, Jesus," Pearl said, smiling.

"I figured you could buy some new clothes and fix the house up a little bit."

"Wait a minute . . . where did you really get this money from?" Pearl grew suspicious and glanced at his right hand.

Spaz stuffed the blood stained bills in his pocket, keeping his hand out of her sight. "I told you. I found it in the couch. It was all the way near the bottom. I dropped the last of my change in there and had to go digging for it." Spaz smiled. "Maybe Pops hid this in there before he got knocked."

"Yeah maybe, but I still feel like something's fishy about this money. You bet not have robbed nobody for this."

"Mom, take it easy. I found it, okay?"

"Well, here, you can use some of the money for yourself." She handed him some of the cash back.

"No ma'am, that is yours." Spaz headed toward the bedroom door. "I'll wash the rest and give 'em to you when they're dry."

"Your father been calling here all day to speak to you." Pearl folded up the money.

"For real? Damn, I missed his call. I can't wait for him to get outta that place."

"Oh lord, you don't know how much I feel the same way," said Pearl.

"I spoke with him yesterday. How does he know everything that goes on, on the streets while being locked up?"

"Like what?"

"He just be knowing stuff. He told me to stay away from Reel."

"Drug dealing Reel?" she said, hoping that she was mistaken.

"Yeah, he's cool with me."

"Listen to me," she said in a serious manner, pointing her finger. "Do not go around him. That man is the devil. You hear me?"

"A'ight."

"Don't a'ight me, Giovanni. Promise me you will stay away from him."

"Okay, I promise," he said, walking back to hug his mom.

Spaz headed out of Pearl's room with a nagging feeling in his gut. He only lied to her when necessary, but it still didn't feel right. Spaz only hoped that no one he trusted would lie to him at any time for any reason. Especially Grams and Slugger. He wondered what he'd do if either of them ever lied to him.

Federal Agent Mark Rizzo and his fellow officers paced the floor of his small apartment drinking beers and listening to Rizzo complain.

"Fuck! Where is this guy? He was our only key witness to the Black Boss Family."

"He probably skipped town, or maybe he is . . . how do they say it? Laying low?" He held up a folder with some papers inside. "You see this? This is enough to put Reel away for life."

"Who the hell does Reel think he is? He couldn't be happy with his dirty drug money. He decides to start programs to help the ghetto kids. And now Chips is missing."

"Well, we know about his next shipment. We can get him on possession with attempt to deliver, and most likely he will have a gun on him. That's possession of a firearm without a license. This shipment, plus his parole violation, will put him away for the rest of his life."

"You know what? You're absolutely right. I think it's time to pay Mr. Reel a visit."

I can't fuck this up. **Spaz strolled up the street.** "Man, we need some cars. All this walking is hurting my feet."

Spaz, Grams, and Slugger walked toward the buildings that Chips used to manage. Reel gave Spaz the buildings to run.

"Real rap," Grams said, watching a Cadillac race up the block.

They walked along Twenty-fifth Street, one of the many dangerous blocks in North Philly. Slugger carried the Gucci gym bag that Reel gave them.

"So where were you last night? I was calling you like crazy," Grams said.

"Reel gave me a bottle of Henny. I was fucked up at the crib. My mom had to come help me off the kitchen floor." The crew burst out in laughter.

"Me and Slugger was celebrating, popping bottles at this bitch crib. Nigga, I seen Chips on Channel 7 News, dead than a bitch. When the police said no suspects, we started popping bottles and wilding out," Grams said, proud of killing Chips.

"This shit is real!" Spaz said.

"You right, partner, and because of you we gone be rich this summer," Slugger said, carrying the gym bag strapped over his shoulders. Grams and Spaz guarded him with their guns off safety.

"You already know!" Spaz responded. He conceitedly looked at his reflection off the parked cars as he walked past.

Slugger noticed a group of gangsters on the corner of Twenty-fifth and Thompson. "I don't fuck with these niggas from up here. They is grimy," Slugger said. "This is not even our territory." He noticed a young thug eyeing his Gucci bag as they walked by.

Grams grew over protective. "Man, fuck these niggas. I'll clap anybody!" He looked at the group of thugs with no intimidation. *I wish one of you bitch ass nigga would act like they got a problem.*

"You got a light?" one of the thugs asked.

"No, but I got a bullet," Grams mumbled.

"We don't smoke. We just say no to drugs," said Spaz. *Ain't nobody stopping to give you niggas no light. We got over twenty thousand dollars' worth of crack in this gym bag.* He watched for any sudden movements of the criminals that watched them like a hawk.

Spaz called Maine, whose phone rang a few times before he answered. "Yerrrr," Maine said.

"Maine, this Spaz. We turning the corner now. Come outside." Spaz hung up the phone as they turned up Thompson Street.

Maine was a hustler who boxed at the Knock-Out gym in North Philly. He was a stocky guy around 5-feet 8-inches tall. He wore a goatee and short hair usually covered by a baseball cap that he kept low over his eyes. Maine got initiated and was made a full-blooded BBF member after he beat Big Pete to death in an abandoned house. Just like Spaz, Maine killed and connived his way to the top. He was known as Chips' young He-Man. Chips and Maine had plans to corner the drug market, but when Cash got killed, Reel was made Boss.

Spaz stared at the tall building and walked through its entrance. *Who the fuck is that?* He noticed a thug with a gun by his waist. He stood there with a baseball cap tilted over his eyes. His shoulders looked like he had on shoulder pads.

"You Spaz?" asked Maine, trying to intimidate Spaz.

"Yeah, you Maine?"

"Yeah, I'm him."

"Why you got your fuckin' gun out then?" asked Spaz.

"You never know where you might bump into an enemy at," he said, puffing on a cigarette.

"You going to put that gun up, or do I got to pull out mine?" said Spaz.

Grams pulled out his gun.

"Easy, cowboy, I don't want no trouble. You said Reel sent you, right?" asked Maine.

"You already know." Spaz was getting frustrated.

"Follow me," Maine said, leading the way up the staircase. It was filled with addicts walking around looking for drugs.

"Y'all muthafuckas line up and shut the fuck up!" Maine said, arriving on the second floor hallway. "Follow me, gentlemen," he said, walking to room 201. He opened the door and entered a room.

Storm was getting head from a decent looking crack head. "Yo, man. Why you didn't knock?" he said, pulling his dick out of Marlene's mouth. "Cock blocking muthafuckas!" He pulled up his pants and adjusted his belt.

Storm was crazy as all out doors. He started off robbing dice games. But when he shot-up Dante in his car for disrespecting Chips, he got initiated into the Black Boss Family. "So what's up? These the new niggas Reel sent up here?"

"Yeah, we the new niggas that Reel sent up here. I'm Spaz. This is Grams. And Slugger. Pleased to fuckin' meet you, too. Now, can we get to business?"

Who the fuck he think he talking to? "So you got to be Spaz because you sound so spazy." He laughed.

"Where the coke at?" said Maine.

"It is right here," Spaz said, pointing at the gym bag. Slugger opened the bag, exposing thousands of nickel bags of crack.

"Okay, let me put you on game. The crack heads out there love this coke. They a do anything for it. It's so many crack heads that live here and buy, that you going to be finished with that by tonight," Maine said.

Twenty fucking thousand? "Oh okay, that's what's up," Spaz replied.

"Bring a couple of bundles out here," Maine said, walking out the room.

Spaz grabbed some bundles out the gym bag and followed Maine. Grams and Slugger followed Spaz and Storm followed Grams and Slugger.

The staircase was packed with crack fiends. "Now listen up, we need one straight line. We got them boulders bigger than your shoulders," Maine said, using his promotion pitch. The fiends lined up one by one. Spaz stood at the top of the staircase serving long lines of fiends.

"Let me get five! Let me get six nickel bags! Let me get ten!" was all Spaz heard from five different customers.

"One at a time, one at a time!" Spaz screamed.

Maine and Storm watched from a distance.

Spaz and his boys moved as a unit.

"Them niggas don't know what they doing," Maine said. "Reel on that bullshit, sending this nigga Spaz up here to run the buildings. Like he gone be underboss or something," Maine said to Storm.

"You already know Reel is shifty. If Chips was alive, I'd rather him be boss instead of Reel's muscle-head ass," said Storm, watching as Spaz stuffed money in his pocket.

"That nigga is nobody. I remember when we was in school. I used to smack him around and take his lunch money," Storm said.

"Man, fuck those niggas. They not even gone last long around here anyway. They food for the wolves. I'm the next king around this muthafucka," Maine said, adjusting his gun on his waist.

On the corner of Thompson Street was a gold mine. The small drug-infested motel was like crack head central. From that day on, Spaz, Slugger, and Grams dropped out of school and worked twenty-four hour shifts. Slugger would work for six hours, then Grams would take over for another six hours and so on and so forth.

Hood riches would take some time to acquire, that much they knew. It would, however, eventually be within their reach if business moved the way it had today, and as long as haters like Maine played his position.

Chapter Six
SMELLS LIKE MONEY

Six months ago . . .
"Excuse me, ma'am," Reel had said, squeezing between two people as he stepped down an upward escalator. "Excuse me, sir," he said, knocking an older man off balance. Reel made it down to the first floor level.

The very attractive female switched her hips from side to side, looking stunning in a Chanel dress that hugged her body like a latex glove. Her five thousand dollar Fendi boots tap danced on the Gallery Mall floors. She slowed down and stared at some jewelry through the glass, hoping Reel would catch up to her. Vanessa had always crushed on muscular, dark-skinned men.

"Excuse me. My name is Reel," he said as the breeze blew the fragrance of his Polo cologne up her nostrils.

Mmm, he smells so good. Vanessa smiled. "Nice to meet you." *Smells just like money.*

"Baby, did you know we've been together six months already?" Vanessa said, briefly stealing a glance at Reel's handsome face while she drove. Reel was worried about getting pulled over by the police. The weird feeling in his chest didn't make the trip any better, but he tried to relax anyway.

"It's been six months already? Damn, time be flying."

"Aww, it feels like I've known you forever. You're like my soul mate, daddy."

A few minutes later, she parked in front of the apartment buildings in South Philly on Twenty-fourth and Snyder. She smiled, and they shared each other's tongue and lips. "I love you," Vanessa said.

"You my Bonnie, and I'm your Clyde. Let me handle this business," Reel said as he pulled out his cell phone and dialed Chris Cannon's number. "I'm outside," he said.

"Say no more, youngster," Cannon said. He was forty-five years old and he stood 6-feet 1-inch tall and 188 pounds. Chris Cannon was an old school player, who looked like Goldie from *The Mack.* Cannon relocated from his mother's house on Parish Street in North Philly, to the Wilson Projects Homes with his baby's mother in South Philly. There, he created a five thousand dollar per day trap spot. His reputation grew so strong that he was given the green light from Cash to start up a BBF headquarters in South Philly.

Cannon approached Reel's truck wearing a white chinchilla mink coat. "What up, player? I see you shining, baby. Pop the trunk so I can load you up."

Reel ordered Vanessa to pop the trunk, and Cannon signaled one of his workers to drop a bag filled with cocaine inside. Reel gave Cannon a brown paper bag with $100,000 inside, all one hundred-dollar bills.

"Oh yeah, good looking out on that situation about Chips trying to cut a side deal. He's been running his mouth. I found out he was snitching," Reel said in a low tone so Vanessa couldn't hear him. "He's history now. They'll never find his body."

Cannon shook Reel's hand. "Listen here, youngster. In 1988 I got busted with four keys. It was my second offense, but I had a high-powered lawyer who got me fifty months, which was good for the record I had." Cannon noticed Vanessa's cleavage and loved the way her tits jiggled when she moved. "I never told on nobody, and I never will. I can do my time just like you would do yours. I am true to the game, not new to the game, youngster."

Reel smiled. "That's what I'm talking about . . . I'll see you in a week." He glanced around the perimeter, making sure he wasn't being followed.

"Relax, daddy. I got ya back," Vanessa told Reel as she rubbed his shoulder. "I would've told you if a tail was on us. I would've seen it." She glanced around as well, trying to make him feel comfortable. It didn't work. Reel had bubble guts.

"Let's just get outta here," he said, damn near holding his breath.

On high alert, Vanessa drove Reel back to Philly with the kilos neatly wrapped in plastic and duct taped inside of the trunk. The two made it safely to Reel's condo in the suburbs, and Reel gave a sigh of relief. He exited the car and stretched his legs. Vanessa opened the trunk, and Reel reached in to grab the bag. With so much on Reel's mind, he didn't notice Vanessa reaching in her purse and pulling out a Glock .40.

"Freeze, Reel! Put the bag down and your face on the ground. Now!"

Reel punched Vanessa in the jaw. The hard blow knocked Vanessa and her gun to the ground. He ran for the gun, and the two indulged in a wrestling match for possession of the firearm. Within seconds, five police cars quickly raced up Reel's driveway.

Agent Mark Rizzo and his boys jumped out their cars aiming their weapons. "Freeze, Reel! Get down! Get down!"

Reel put his hands up. "I should have known," he said.

"Keep your hands up, Reel," Vanessa said, not really wanting to do her job.

"All this time you was a cop? A cop!" Reel swung a quick hard punch that landed on Vanesa's jaw. The loud punch twisted her jaw and impacted her brain. She dropped her gun and fell to the ground unconscious.

Mark Rizzo rushed Reel like a corner back from the NFL and tackled him to the hard concrete. Reel tussled with three officers as Rizzo began handcuffing him. "You're lucky it's too many nappy-headed witnesses watching us because I would kill your black ass!" said Rizzo, squeezing the handcuffs so tight on Reel's wrists that they bled and swelled instantly.

"These cuffs are too tight!" Reel complained.

"Shut up!" Rizzo shouted. He and his officers roughly escorted Reel to the patrol car.

Reel ducked his head from the news camera. A crowd of neighbors gathered, and an ambulance pulled up to the scene.

Vanesa lay on the ground, regaining consciousness.

"You slimy maggot bitch! I trusted you, 'ho! I'll be out before dinner, muthafucka!" said Reel.

"It's getting cold out this bitch," Spaz said, walking toward the front door of his mom's house after exiting a yellow cab with Grams and Slugger. The cab sped away up the avenue. Spaz and Grams held their hands close to their guns securing Slugger, who carried the Gucci gym bag that Reel gave them.

"Yo, y'all got to be quiet. My mom's probably in there sleep," said Spaz, unlocking the front door. "Come on," he said. They followed Spaz into his basement and placed the bag on an old pool table.

Spaz's cell phone rang. He looked at the number twice, but knew he should answer once he saw the words Federal Prison on the display. "Hello?"

"You have a collect call from . . . Reel," said the operator. Spaz heard the words clearly, as if Reel were standing in front of him.

"Yo, I'm locked up," Reel yelled.

"You what!"

"I need you and Maine to come see me on Thursday. Get up here early!" Reel said. "I need you to go to the *spiznot* and get that *piznaper*. Get the key from my sister. Tell her I sent you."

Spaz deciphered the codes that Reel spoke. *Go to the stash house and get the money to pay for his lawyer.*

"Say no more, old head. I got you," he said, hanging up the phone.

"What happened?" said Grams.

"Yeah, nigga, don't leave us in the dark," asked Slugger.

"The Feds got Reel."

"Damn!" said Grams.

"I guess we on our own now," Spaz answered.

The stash house was located on 909 Corinthian Avenue, a quiet block on the outskirts of the hood. Spaz drove to his destination and saw FBI agents swarming in and out of Reel's stash house. He kept driving as if he didn't see anything at all, riding by and blending in with traffic.

Federal agent Mark Rizzo stepped into Reel's stash house with his gun drawn. *I know he got some cash in here.* He searched every room until he stumbled upon a monopoly box. It was odd for it to be hidden under a mattress. He opened it. *Holy shit!* A monopoly box filled to the top with crispy one-hundred dollar bills. Rizzo quickly started stuffing cash in his pants, pockets, socks, and down his underwear. *Another day on the job!*

Chapter Seven
BELLY OF THE BEAST

"There he go right there," said Maine to Spaz while pointing at Reel as he entered the visit area.

"Aww shit, look at old head." Spaz smiled.

Reel strolled past inmates seated with their visits. He noticed Spaz and Maine. "Yerrr!" he said, then walked in their direction. Spaz stood up and hugged Reel.

"Group hug, nigga," Reel joked as Maine showed his respects by hugging and shaking Reel's hand.

"What's up, OG?" Maine said, then they all got seated.

"What the fuck happened?" asked Spaz.

"Man, they got me. They got me good. That bitch set me up."

"Who? The white j'awn?" asked Maine.

"Yup, she was an undercover cop."

"Aww, that's crazy!" Spaz shook his head in disbelief.

"I'm fucked. They got all the stash spots, the plug, and Cannon locked up. It's looking bad for me, fam'." Reel was upset. "I'm just in this jail for a gun charge I had, but my lawyer said the Feds will come get me afterward."

"You just make sure you stay strong. We gone get you outta here, no matter if we got to blaze you out this bitch," said Spaz.

"What your lawyer talking about? He wouldn't tell me shit," Maine said.

"I'm looking at a long ass time, fam'. That bitch knew everything. I should a known better! Damn!" he said, clapping his hands and releasing anger. "But I'm going to need more money for lawyers and appeal lawyers, nigga. We still got to keep the BBF running. Now the bitch know too much, but one thing she don't know is Spaz."

Reel directed his attention to Spaz. "I know I told you to keep that twenty grand, but I need you to give that to my lawyer."

"I got you," Spaz said, looking disappointed.

"Don't worry about it. Any drugs you get your hands on, I'm going to let you sell it in the buildings, anytime you want."

"What? This young, wet-behind-the-ears ass nigga? You can't be serious!" Maine said, pointing at Spaz with his thumb.

"Watch your mouth, nigga," Spaz said, giving Maine a dead ass serious expression.

"Why? What you gone do, nigga?"

"You two be cool. Can y'all please settle y'all differences for me? I really need this money, so y'all gone have to work together."

"This is some nut ass shit! So what you want us to do, Reel?"

Reel moved closer to them and spoke in a low tone. "Everybody locked up. That fucking crooked ass cop took two hundred thousand out my spot. The police caught me on tape buying ten keys, my nigga. This shit going to end up turning federal, and I wanted y'all to come see me because when the alphabet boys come, they gonna ship me somewhere far." He turned to Spaz.

"Listen, young boy, you keep doing what you do, and you going to be a boss. You went from a man to the man! Remember, trust no one—not even God. You gone have to hold it down. Shit is hot, my nigga," said Reel.

"You know I'm going to hold you down. You put me on my feet," Spaz said, glancing at Maine.

The three stood and gave each other handshakes.

"We on it," said Maine without conviction, looking off to the right. *I'm not dying for none of you motherfuckers!*

A year passed, and Reel's big trial was in two hours, and Mark Rizzo was going to enjoy seeing his head under the gavel.

This was Agent Rizzo's ninth year on the FBI. He felt like a celebrity in a new movie the way cameras flashed and how crowded the court room was. *Why did Reel invite all his family here just to see him get hung by a jury?*

Judge Bobrick ushered the prosecutor to begin. Ms. Limbo was responsible for presenting the case in this criminal trial.

"Your Honor," she said, "we have here the United States of America versus Reel Ocean."

Judge Bobrick stared at Reel with disdain.

The prosecutor rose to her feet. "Your Honor, on Friday, January twenty-second, our agent, Vanessa Drumlin witnessed Mr. Ocean buy ten kilos of cocaine from South Philly kingpin, Chris Cannon. We arrested Mr. Ocean and Mr. Cannon. We confiscated guns and large quantities of cocaine, which they manufactured and distributed through the streets of Philadelphia. Twenty other members of the Black Boss Family were indicted on drug charges as well. We have proof that Mr. Ocean is the leader and main supplier of the Black Boss Family."

The evidence was too obvious, making it hard for Reel's lawyer to convince the jury that he was innocent. *This cracker is going to bury me. If it wasn't for Spaz making these moves for me on the streets, I would be broke.* Reel held back his rage, hoping the judge would be lenient on him.

Reel was responsible for a lot of lives that were taken away by senseless acts of violence. No murders were ever charged against him, because no one had the courage to talk to the police. But there was one guy who didn't care. He was in rage sitting behind Reel and watching the trial. His name was Clarence and he was Chips' father.

Clarence got a phone call from Chips the day of his murder. *"Hello?"*

"Dad, listen man. I'm scared."

"What?"

"Listen, if anything happens to me, then it was Reel. I gotta go. He coming."

Dial tone.

That was the last conversation he had with his son. Clarence remained silent as the judge began to speak.

"I wish I could go over the sentencing guidelines and give you more time," said Judge Bobrick, raising his voice. "I'm sentencing you to the high end of the guideline of six-hundred months in the federal penitentiary!" He slammed the mallet.

Reel rose to his feet. "Six hundred months for selling drugs? Man, fuck you!" he said, pointing his finger at the judge.

"Get this man out of my courtroom," said Judge Bobrick.

There was tension building in the court room and Clarence was overwhelmed with emotion. He leaped across the table and started choking Reel. "You killed my son!" he said, while squeezing Reel's neck.

Lawyers and prosecutors ran for their lives, while U.S. Marshals quickly removed Clarence from choking Reel.

They apprehended Clarence and placed him under arrest. "You bastard! Ahh!" He was in pain thinking about his son. "You killed my son, you motherfucker. I hope you burn in hell!" he said with tears bursting from his eyes. Blood covered his mouth from tangling with deputies. They placed the handcuffs on him.

Clarence and the BBF got into a shouting match.

"Fuck you, old head!" said Spaz.

"Bring me back my son!" said Clarence.

After the courtroom chaos, deputies cleared the courtroom and dragged the bloody father and Reel out in restraints. Clarence was later released and Reel was left to do six hundred months behind bars.

Chapter Eight
HUNT FOR THE BIG FISH

Satisfied with Reel facing a hefty sentence, next on Agent Mark Rizzo's list was Italian mob boss, Don "Sticky" Scilionni. Sticky Scilionni and his crew killed, robbed, and extorted small businesses. Even though drug dealing was against mafia rules, Sticky was involved in distributing tons of cocaine.

Mark Rizzo was determined to arrest him. He stared at Sticky's mug shot and hated the fact that criminals made more money in a week than he made in a whole year. So he took from them as much as he could. Mark Rizzo rose to his feet and headed out the door.

South Philly was the home of the Italian mob. Mark Rizzo stepped in the Tops-Up Lounge, a bar owned by Sticky Scilionni. He blended in with the crowd, dressed casual and spoke with a strong Italian accent. He ordered a drink, and the bartender greeted him with a glass of Puerto Rican Rum. Rizzo took it straight down the hatch. The place was not that crowded, and there were no signs of Sticky. Just as Agent Rizzo was heading out the door, he noticed a twenty-year-old Italian kid named Tommy Valentine.

Tommy was wanted on gun charges and was Rizzo's source to get information. As Tommy headed out the bar and up the street, Rizzo followed not far behind. He jumped into a Lincoln, headed toward his girlfriend's house, but then noticed Rizzo's unmarked car following him. Tommy pressed his foot on the gas, and Rizzo gave chase. While turning a corner, Tommy lost control of the car and nearly crashed into a fire hydrant. He rolled down his window and threw an ounce of crack cocaine and a .357 Magnum out.

The chase was on and Rizzo called for backup. Rizzo was not giving up and stayed right behind him.

Tommy drove up on a sidewalk, knocking over trashcans. "Oh shit!" he screamed, pressing his foot down on the gas. He regained control and drove off the curb and back onto the street. "Whoooo! You can't catch me!" said Valentine.

"You son of a bitch!" Rizzo said, racing up the block with his sirens blaring. He pressed his foot on the gas, reaching speeds of up to one hundred miles per hour until he crashed into Tommy's rear end, making him spin out of control and into the wall of a South Philadelphia home. The loud crash set off water sprinklers and car alarms.

Twelve-year-old Becky Robinson was sitting at the table playing cards when Valentine's car came crashing through her wall and into her dining room. A piece of the wall pushed her to the floor and fell on top of her. She screamed, feeling her bone crush from her shoulder. She lay buried under bricks and sheet rock.

Tommy's vision was blurry, and the chase was over. He lay slumped over the steering wheel, face bruised, and his nose was bleeding from the impact of the crash.

Agent Rizzo punched him in the face, and then dragged him out of the car.

Tommy nervously sat in the interrogation room inside the Ninth District police headquarters. Mark Rizzo walked in swinging punches that connected to Tommy's jaw. "Motherfucker, you're going to jail for the rest of your life!" Mark Rizzo placed a .357 Magnum and an ounce of crack on the table. "This is why you were trying to get away so bad?"

Tommy was scared to death. Today was a nightmare for him. "Look, man, I didn't mean to hit that little girl."

"Oh, you didn't! You know what? I am a proud Sicilian, and you, my friend, give our people a bad name. I know you are in the Scilionni family, and I know about your drug dealing. You're in a lot of trouble, Mr. Valentine. You hit that little girl, and if she dies, you're going to be behind bars for the rest of your little miserable life! Now help yourself by telling me something about Sticky Scilionni."

Tommy felt like a mouse in a trap. "Sticky who? I never heard of him! I want my lawyer in here, right now!"

"Is that right? I will have you in jail so long that when you get out, your grandchildren will have grandkids!"

"Look, man, I don't know Sticky!"

"Stop lying to me! You know what I'm going to leave your sorry ass here to rot! I'll be back here tomorrow afternoon. If you don't give me something good, I am going to make sure you share a cell with Joey the butt lover!" Agent Rizzo stormed out the door.

Sticky Scilionni and underboss Nikki Montagna talked business at a nearby bowling alley. Both men held their hands over their mouths so no cameras could read their lips. They also talked low so audio could not catch their conversation.

"Sticky, Tommy Valentine got pinched a couple hours ago. He ran over some poor little girl while getting chased by the cops. She's in critical condition for Christ's sake," said Montagna.

Sticky frowned. "I used to lay pipe to his mother." Sticky lit up a cigarette and blew smoke in the air. "You think he would give us up?" He stared into his underboss' eyes, waiting for an answer.

Nikki Montagna knew that his answer would determine the life of Tommy Valentine. Nikki's decision was made. "Why take a chance?" he replied.

Sticky grew concerned. "How much is his bail?"

"One hundred thousand big-ones," said Montagna.

"This fuckin' guy." Sticky shook his head in a rage.

Tommy Valentine sat in a lonely cell crying. Sheriffs walked to his cage.

"Hey, asshole, you made bail!"

Tommy grew confused. "I did?"

Mark Rizzo walked through the police district, showed his badge, and demanded to see Tommy Valentine.

"Tommy Valentine got bailed out early this morning."

"Why didn't anybody notify me? Goddammit! He was the key to unlock the case on Sticky Scilionni, and you fucking guys just let him out!"

Sticky and Nikki Montagna walked into the basement of Tops-Up Lounge with Tommy following behind. Sticky turned toward Tommy and noticed the bruises on his face. "Tommy, your face looks terrible. Did the cops rough you up?"

"Oh no, this came from the car accident."

"How could you be so stupid?"

"Sticky, it was a mistake."

"You can't afford to make mistakes! What did the cops ask you?"

"They didn't ask me anything."

"You are lying! What did you tell them?"

Tommy began crying after Nikki Montagna pulled his gun out and held it by his side. "I didn't say anything, Sticky. Please don't do it!"

Nikki aimed his .357 at Tommy's head. "You fucking prick!" He pulled the trigger with no remorse. One shot blew Tommy's head in thirty directions.

Sticky looked down at him. "Cut his tongue out and send it to his fucking mother! He would have ended up being a rat."

For the next several weeks, Federal Agent Mark Rizzo went into a state of depression. He barely ate or used the phone. He drove his car seventy miles per hour until he reached Tenth and Chestnut, then parked. He headed into Children's Hospital, raced to the elevator and pushed the button for the eighth floor. After twenty seconds of deep thought, the elevator bell chimed and the doors flew open. Agent Rizzo arrived at Room 118 where the girl's parents sobbed over the devastating news.

Becky's mother broke out in tears. "She's dead. My baby is dead. Oh my God! My baby is gone."

Agent Rizzo punched a hole in the wall from the sight of the little girl lying in an eternal sleep. He felt responsible for her losing her life because of Tommy's reckless driving, and he also felt responsible for the murder of Tommy Valentine. He knew then that nailing Sticky Scilionni would be personal.

Chapter Nine
COINCIDENTAL CONNECTIONS

Sticky Scilionni and Nikki Montagna exited a Jaguar and headed down South Street to the Lennon Shop to get some brand new suits.

"Hey, Sticky. Take a look at them broads over there near the clothing store," Nikki said, knowing Sticky's desire for fine women.

At the sight of an attractive, shapely woman, Sticky was impressed. The female was looking good as ever with curves like the ones a baseball pitcher throws. She wore a tightly fitted Dolce & Gabbana cat suit with a pair of matching stilettos. Her long, silky hair hung down to her back.

The woman walked into a high-end women's retail store with her friend.

"Damn, she is the finest woman I have ever seen in my life," said Sticky, watching one of the women from a distance.

Nikki Montagna noticed Sticky's interest in the taller woman and laughed. "Come on, Sticky. I'm not trying to bust your balls, but we don't have time for chatting."

Those words went in Sticky's right ear and quickly exited the left. Sticky licked his lips and headed toward the door, but stopped at the counter where Pearl laid her new dress. She was counting her money for her dress and was interrupted as Sticky Scilionni stood in front of her.

"Excuse me, I don't mean to interrupt, but you're beautiful."

Pearl smiled from ear to ear. "Thank you."

"Listen, my name is Don Scilionni, but all my friends call me Sticky."

The cashier grew impatient and started to make comments under her breath. "That will be $436."

Pearl stared at her friend Laverne in disbelief as she acknowledged the bad attitude of the cashier. "What is your problem? If you don't like this job, I would suggest you find a better one."

Sticky intervened. "Let me handle this, please." Sticky swiftly reached in his wallet and pulled out five crispy one-hundred-dollar bills. "I will pay the tab here," Sticky said as he gave the cashier the money. "Keep the change, honey. You need it more than I do."

Laverne and Pearl looked at each other and began laughing.

Nikki Montagna stared in disbelief and muttered, "This fucking guy."

Pearl and Sticky headed out the store in a deep conversation.

"You didn't have to pay for my dress."

"Forget about it."

"Well, thank you, Don."

"It was my pleasure to buy that beautiful dress for you. Maybe I might be lucky enough to see you wear it one day. So what's your name?"

"Oh, I am sorry. My name is Pearl."

Sticky and Pearl smiled at each other. Looks of lust dwelled in their eyes.

The next several weeks, Pearl and Sticky engaged in many romantic nights. One special evening, the two counted the stars from the balcony of the Ritz-Carlton Hotel. The room was polished with decorations and a calm invitation for lovemaking. Pearl and Sticky stared at the beautiful view, sipping on champagne.

"Sticky, this is beautiful."

Sticky stared into her eyes. "You're beautiful."

Pearl felt herself getting moist as their lips touched. The wet kiss sparked the mood. Sticky began to remove her clothes and carried her to the bedroom.

"I love you," Pearl said. *I can't believe I just said that.*

"I love you too," said Sticky. "And if you ever cheat on me I'll fucking kill ya!" He laughed.

After another romantic night, morning arrived way too soon for the love struck couple. The two showered and dressed and made plans for another date later that week.

Pearl sat in the passenger side of Sticky's new Mercedes Benz. She thought, *I must be trippin' to let him drop me off in front of my house. He must have me whipped. I'll have to make this quick before my son pulls up on us and starts asking me a thousand questions.*

"Well, you take care of that lovely body." Sticky reached in his pocket and pulled out a few hundred dollars. "Here, take this cash for your groceries."

Pearl smiled. "Thank you, boo. I will call you later tonight." She exited the car and headed into her house. Pearl peeked out the curtains and watched Sticky drive off. *I'm so crazy about this man! Shit, I'm in love!* She blushed.

Pearl was dumbfounded after realizing how deep her feelings had developed for Sticky. And even though

Sticky may have said he would kill her for cheating in a joking manner, she knew he was dead serious.

Chapter Ten
MY BABY BOY IS GROWN

Hypnotized by the idea of falling in love, Pearl was still gazing out her window long after Sticky had pulled off. Spaz stood behind her.

"Oh my God!" Pearl dropped her handbag in shock and turned to face her son. "Spaz, you scared the shit out of me!"

Spaz smiled. "What you doing with that Italian nigga?"

"Listen, Spaz, I am grown."

"I know, Mom. I'm just asking a question. He looks like a Mafioso motherfucka."

"Watch ya mouth, boy. I'm still your mother."

Their conversation was interrupted by the telephone.

Spaz stared at the house phone. "I shouldn't even answer this shit," he complained. Finally he decided to answer the phone. "Hello?"

"You have a call from a federal correctional facility. To accept this call push five, to decline please hang up now," said the recorded message.

Spaz pushed five. "Hey Dad. What's the deal?"

Flash felt relieved to hear his son's voice. "Nothing much, son. I'm trying to keep my head above water. A lot of things have been on my mind lately."

"Like what? What's going on?"

"What you're out there doing in those streets is what's going on. Just like the streets talk, I hear a lot of shit in here, too."

Spaz sighed.

"Yeah, I know you don't want to hear it, but listen, son. The game doesn't love anyone. Trust me when I tell you to get what you can and get out while you still have a chance."

Spaz walked upstairs into his bedroom for privacy. "Dad, what the hell are you talking about? I can't leave the game alone. Are you crazy?"

"No, I'm not crazy. You don't want to be in here with me, son. This shit is horrible. Your freedom is worth more than money can buy. Many of the cats that I rolled with and so-call friends turned their backs on me as soon as I got locked up. Or you might have another problem with them snitching on you."

"Me and my crew are immune to snitchin'. I'm not worried about that at all."

"Same thing I thought. Spaz, I will be home next month, and I'm telling you now, if I have to give my life to save yours then I will do that."

Spaz stood in his bedroom in disbelief. He couldn't believe his father planned to leave the game and insisted that he quit his business as well. "Listen, Pop, I'm not going to talk too much on this phone, but I'm in too deep, and quitting is not an option."

"I don't have much time left on the phone anyway. We will talk later. Put your mom on the phone."

Spaz walked downstairs to the living room and gave his mother the phone.

She smiled and pressed the phone to her ear. "Hello?"

"What's up, gorgeous?"

"How are you doing, baby? I miss you."

"Guess what, baby?"

"What?"

"Today I signed the paperwork to come home."

Pearl grew silent.

"Baby, I thought you would be happy for me?"

"Of course I am happy, baby."

"I know you been doing your thing, but I want you to cut all that shit off."

Her mind instantly reverted to her intimate evening with Sticky.

"Okay, baby, I got to go. My phone time is over. I'll call you Tuesday."

"Okay, baby, I love you." Pearl began to cry. She called her best friend Lavern for advice.

After a couple days, Pearl reached the conclusion that she was going to end her relationship with Sticky. Although she loved the gifts, the romantic nights, and the lovemaking, she had to end the fling. She contemplated if she could let it go, and she thought about how Sticky would feel when she gave him the news. Pearl wondered if she should be afraid. Sticky was, after all, a high ranking Mafia figure.

A month passed and Pearl was on her way to the hotel to meet Sticky. It was hard for her to explain the situation to Sticky, because each time she would open her mouth to speak about it, somehow they ended up making love. Sticky's lifestyle was impressive. His fancy suits and hotel suites made Pearl happy.

She walked into a hotel room covered with red rose petals that had her initials engraved in each one. Sticky told Pearl how special she was to him, and he wanted to keep her in his corner forever. Once again they had passionate sex and fell asleep.

The next morning, Sticky and Pearl were in a deep sleep. Sticky awoke from the loud ringing of her cell phone, stumbled to his feet, and began scratching his head as he picked up her phone. Sometimes it rang at all hours of the night. Sticky told her the next time it rang he would answer it. Now that the opportunity was present, he decided to answer the call since the two had gotten so close. Sticky was falling in love with her and did not want anyone to interfere.

He glanced back at Pearl sleeping soundly and picked the phone up. "Hello?" Sticky frowned after hearing a recorded message from prison. He pushed five. "Hello?"

Flash grew angry hearing another man's voice answering Pearl's phone. "Yo, who the hell is this, and where is my wife?"

Sticky's lips tightened. "Your wife? Sure, hold on for a second." Sticky looked down at Pearl lying fast asleep on the bed. He grew aroused watching her, so he pressed himself up against her naked body, and entered her. She woke up, moaning in pure pleasure. Sticky held the cell phone in the air.

Flash's heart dropped when he heard his wife getting fucked.

Sticky grinned with the devil beaming in his eyes. "You still want to speak with her, you cocksucker?"

"What the hell are you doing?" Pearl grew hysterical after realizing what Sticky had done. "Why did you answer my phone?"

"Forget about it."

She snatched the phone out of his hand and looked at the caller ID. "Oh shit! How could you invade my privacy?" Pearl began crying loudly and shouting several times, "I can't believe you did that!"

Sticky put his clothes on. "Well, believe it, honey!" he said and barged out the door.

Chapter Eleven
WE MADE IT!

The key thirteen members of the Black Boss Family gathered at the neighborhood schoolyard.

Spaz rose to his feet. "I would like to first thank you all for coming. Your appearance shows me your loyalty. Reel just got a cell phone that we gave to our inside connect. He gone be calling any minute to lay down the law."

"And we all know who really run shit," said Maine.

"I'm not saying I run shit, bro," said Spaz, trying not to lose his cool.

"You acting like you boss already," Maine replied.

"I made me and my crew twenty racks last month. I'm good with numbers, and I bust my gun at any given time. I set it up for Reel to receive weed, syrup, mollies, and a cell phone in jail. From a correctional officer that I hunted down off of Facebook. Nigga, I been getting money. Where the fuck you been?"

"Nigga, you still wet behind the ears. What the fuck you know about being a boss?"

"I'm a star, motherfucker," said Spaz

Spaz's ringing cell phone broke up the argument.

"Yo, what's up, big homie?" said Spaz.

"Everybody there?" Reel replied.

"Yeah," said Spaz.

"Okay, put me on speaker."

Spaz put his phone on speaker and BBF members gathered around.

"Yo, I been sitting up here thinking about this for a while, and I made my decision on the next boss of the family. I exhausted my appeal rights, and it looks like I will be seventy years old when I get out. I want everyone to respect my decision. I don't want this crew to ever turn their backs on each other, and no one . . . I mean no one is to be executed without my fucking permission." He paused. "Maine will be underboss and Spaz is the new boss of the BBF." Some dissent ensued among the members. "Yo. Y'all chill with all the mumbling and back talk and let me explain."

"Yo, won't y'all shut the fuck up and let him finish," said Cola, bumping Princess on the arm.

"Yeah, this better be good, Reel," Maine said, glaring at Spaz.

"The reason I chose Spaz is because he proved his loyalty; he proved his heart; he proved his financial strategies to keep the family flowing. He has the potential to take over the whole city. And he's under the radar unlike most of you niggas."

"Man, fuck this shit!" Maine said, storming off toward his car.

"Wait for me!" said Storm as he followed.

BBF members watched as Maine and Storm burned rubber up the block.

"Where Maine at?" Reel asked. "Did that nigga leave?"

"Yeah," a few members said. "He stepped off. He feeling some type of way."

"Don't worry about him. I'll take care of it, but yo, I need a nice check from every one of y'all every month. Get money and fuck bitches! BBF nigga!"

"BBF!" yelled every member.

"I'm a holla at y'all later. Hold it the fuck down! And Spaz, don't let us down, nigga." Reel hung up the phone.

Spaz began to speak. "I have to put together a plan for our wealth to continue. Since we lost Reel and all of his connections, we are low on suppliers of coke. We need some better connections."

Grams rose to his feet. "How are we going to do it? No one has cocaine as pure as Reel's shit. Everyone else has garbage!"

Spaz rubbed his chin. "We got to get this money."

Grams took a hit of his blunt. "Everyone here is willing to ride for you, and we will kill anybody anywhere, anytime for you, my nigga. We know that you would do the same thing for us!"

Spaz hit the weed a couple times. "It's a new time. We can't afford to lose. This era calls for us to ride, not die! In any case, we must understand that even in death our memory will never be forgotten. We must maintain our status on the streets and continue to get money. We are going to ride on all these motherfuckers!"

The Black Boss Family agreed as Slugger rose to his feet. "I have a new connection for some good coke from my new Puerto Rican mommy's brother from the Badlands. We all know the Ricans are known for having the best powder. We can take that shit and cook it up and get back to business."

Spaz shook his head in agreement

"I'm on it," Slugger said, nodding his head.

"Ay Slugger? Did Reel forget all about us?" Princess said as she and Cola walked toward him.

"Ask Spaz. I don't know," Slugger responded, heading toward Grams.

The two females began approaching Spaz to see what Reel set in motion for them.

"He just forgot all about us," Princess said to Cola.

"What you mean?" Cola asked.

"He told them to get money and fuck bitches, but he forgot to tell us to get money and get niggas," Princess said and then chuckled.

"As long as it's a boss nigga with money, I wouldn't mind at all." Cola said, keeping Spaz within her eyesight.

"I feel you, girl," Princess said, peeping at Spaz briefly as they finally stood near him.

Slugger set up the deal. Spaz drove his Lexus up Broad Street with Slugger and Grams. The rest of his gang followed in separate cars. All the cars pulled over on a small block in the Badlands. This was an exclusive Puerto Rican neighborhood infested with drugs and crime. Most people were scared to drive through this neighborhood. The Black Boss Family wasn't. The family came prepared for war. Each man was strapped with a weapon. Spaz exited the car and popped the trunk. He pulled out a Louis Vuitton gym bag with $125,000 inside.

Another car pulled up the block and the Royal Crown gang exited their vehicles. The leader's name was Bert, who got his reputation from doing hits for a thousand dollars. He approached Spaz, and his gang followed closely behind.

"What's up, papi?" Slugger and Bert shook hands.

"You got the money?" Bert asked Spaz.

"I wouldn't be here if I didn't have the money." Spaz was instantly offended.

"Slow down, man. Take it easy. I got the work right here, man." Bert pulled out a backpack with five kilos inside.

Spaz's eyes grew wide as he handed Bert the bag of money. Bert gave Spaz the bag of drugs. All the gangsters were feeling the tension in the air. Spaz and his gang began to back up as Spaz tasted the coke. Bert and his men moved smoothly as Bert counted the money. Bert immediately noticed the serial numbers on the money were all the same. He grew suspicious and then spit on one of the hundred-dollar bills, and it turned green with ink running off of it.

"You fucking piece of shit! This is fake money!" Bert pulled out a Desert Eagle and started shooting at Spaz.

Spaz ducked and took cover, pulling out his weapon. The shots multiplied as the Black Boss Family and the Royal Crowns began having a shootout in broad daylight.

Both gangs escaped to the opposite side of the narrow street. They took shelter behind parked cars and bus stops. A young thug from the Royal Crown gang raised his head from behind the trunk of a car. With a look of aggression, he aimed and fired ten explosive shots and returned to his position behind the Pontiac.

"I'ma kill you, motherfucker!" Bert roared like a lion. His gun thumped five times, sending hollow points directly at Spaz.

Sparks lit up his surroundings behind a pickup truck. He stayed low, keeping bullets from striking him, realizing that his life depended on it. "I got something for you, Bert!" Spaz sent eleven shots in Bert's direction.

"Oh shit!" Bert was dormant until a hollow point whistled past his face. "Ha! You missed me, papi!"

Bert's associates returned fire, shattering car windows as a body lay in front of Spaz. "Get up, nigga!" he screamed to a BBF member, watching his dying body shake on the cold concrete.

"Damn!" said Spaz, blasting his gun, hoping to hit Bert.

Slugger reloaded his clip and waited for the perfect time. His eyes focused on a Royal Crown member who did a terrible job at shielding himself, which was essential in a moment like this. Slugger hunted his prey like a cheetah chasing a herd of buffalos. His plan was to shoot through the broken window. If his theory was correct, he would be able to fill the young thug with hot slugs.

Slugger pulled his trigger and struck his target in the face and chest. "I got that motherfucker!" he said, watching his victim fall flat-out on the curb bleeding.

The Black Boss Family found themselves outnumbered, outgunned, and low on ammo.

"Ay yo, Bert? I didn't know this was fake money!" Spaz pleaded.

"Okay, I believe you!" Bert said, opening fire. A bullet ricocheted off the stop sign.

Grams shot the last two bullets from his gun. He crawled to the Lexus with bullets flying past him, and then he got the front door open and pushed the trunk button. He gripped the handle of his AR-15 assault rifle.

Bert knew Spaz and his gang were outnumbered, and now was his time to kill them all. Bert said, "Out of bullets?" while walking toward the Black Boss Family's side of the street escorted by seven gunmen releasing gunshots from their weapons. The Black Boss Family began hiding helplessly behind parked cars. "Didn't you know coming down here to the Badlands was suicide!" Bert asked.

"Yo, Bert! You on some bullshit!" Spaz announced.

"Y'all muthafuckas is." Before Bert could finish his statement, Grams sprang upward from between two parked cars, holding his assault rifle. He violently released rapid fire from shoulder level.

Grams' military weapon breathed long flames from its barrel, as small bullets with pointed ends knocked Bert and his gang down like bowling pins.

At that moment Grams thought he was Rambo. He fired his weapon, shaking his arms, flexing his muscles, screaming at the top of his lungs. Grams' reflex capacity allowed him to hit all his targets except for the ones who fled for their lives.

Spaz thought he would never make it out alive until he saw Bert tumble hard to the street with his brains splattered out in front of him. "What the?" he stated, seeing three more dead bodies fall in front of him.

"Come on! Let's go!" Grams yelled, alerting his crew to relinquish their positions.

Slugger crawled from under a parked car and ran toward their vehicles, along with the rest of the surviving members.

Spaz couldn't believe his eyes. "I'm out of here," he said as Grams continued firing.

When the last clips were spent, the Black Boss Family sped away in separate directions.

Spaz laughed. "I got to go through all this for five bricks!"

Chapter Twelve
DEADLY DECISIONS

Pearl sat up in bed reflecting on her relationship with Sticky and came to the conclusion that the father of her child was her true love, and everyone else was just helping her pass time. For weeks Pearl waited by the phone for Flash to call, but he never did. She tried visiting him, but her visits were declined. This rejection made her start to miss Sticky Scilionni, who had called a few times to apologize, but Pearl refused to listen to him.

After several weeks, the two of them reunited, and Sticky continued showering her with gifts. But in the back of her mind she knew Flash was coming home soon, and she would have to end the relationship with Sticky once and for all.

The Scilionni family hung out at the Tops-Up Lounge located on Tenth and Snyder. Outside, it appeared to be a nice upscale place. But those familiar with its inner workings and its owner knew this was a very hostile environment where people were concerned about their next move and worried about getting killed. Sticky was drawn to the flamboyant mob life style and was initiated into the underworld.

Sticky was a made-man, so no one could touch him without permission. He moved up fast in the crime syndicate because of his activities on the streets. This particular day he was sitting in the VIP daydreaming about the Feds arresting him. He felt like somebody had been following him lately, so he began to trace his steps. His thoughts were interrupted by his cell phone. Pearl was calling. He smiled from ear to ear while saying to himself, "I knew she would be calling."

"Sticky, I need to talk to you."

Sticky sensed a problem from the sad tone in her voice. "What's wrong, sweetheart?"

"Can I talk to you in person?"

"Where are you?"

"I'm at Delmonico's restaurant on City Line Avenue."

"Okay, baby, I'll be there. Just calm down."

Pearl sat in the restaurant with tears in her eyes. She knew she had to discontinue the relationship with Sticky, and she finally got enough heart to tell him. She took a deep breath when she saw him pulling up in the parking lot. Pearl had rehearsed what she would say to him. Sticky stepped out of his Mercedes-Benz holding a dozen roses in one hand and smoking a cigar in the other.

Her heart dropped when she saw the roses. *Shit! He is going to make this difficult,* she thought.

Sticky approached Pearl and kissed her cheek. Once he gave her the roses, her conscience started throwing darts at her.

"What's wrong, baby?" Sticky wondered as he took the seat across from her and held her hand and looked her in the eyes. "Baby, what's the problem?"

Tears burst from her eyes. The guilt and shame took over for making the decision not to see him anymore. But with Sticky being so compassionate, she had to come up with something fast and postpone this meeting for another day.

"Sticky, the reason I'm crying and going through such a hard time is because my, my . . . it's because I'm . . ."

Sticky anxiously waited for a response.

At this point she didn't care what she said as long as she said something.

Sticky wiped her tears with his finger. "Come on, baby. Talk to me. Was it something I did?"

Pearl couldn't think of a lie—she was stuck. "Baby, it's . . . It's my son! He is getting into a lot of shit on these streets, and I don't want anything to happen to him. His father is a black man, and my son has no physical resemblance of the Sicilian blood racing through his veins. He's a target like any other young black male. I am so afraid for his life, and I am at a crossroad where I do not know what to do." She felt relieved to finally get a decent story out.

"Forget about it. I'll have a talk with your son and straighten out this situation for you."

She did not think that Sticky would care about her son or offer to help him. "Oh no, Sticky. Don't worry about it."

"Baby, listen. I am going to talk to your son and that's that." He kissed her forehead and stood up to leave.

Pearl cried, staring out the window as Sticky exited the restaurant. *What is Flash going to do when he comes home?*

"Yo, if these motherfuckers don't want to pay up, then we will kill them all! We run this shit! And if anyone steps out of line we will blow their fucking head off!" Spaz yelled, referring to the local drug dealers in North Philly. He puffed on a Dutch Master filled with Philly's finest. He inhaled smoke and blew it out of his nose. Spaz packaged up the bricks he took from Bert and hit the streets hard. Weed heads and crack fiends were lined up to buy 10s, 20s, 50s and 100s. He taxed every drug dealer in the area. He instilled fear into the hearts of many men as he stood in his hood surrounded by his army. He wore all black: Armani jeans, Air Max, and a V-neck T-shirt. The platinum chain around his neck was accompanied by a diamond crusted emblem that read: BBF.

Grams and Slugger watched closely as a Mercedes-Benz parked on the corner. Spaz carefully observed the trespassers with his hand on his gun. The driver side window began to roll down.

Sticky yelled out the window, "Hey, Spaz, come here, kid." Sticky underestimated Spaz, and realized it when he heard numerous guns being cocked back. "Whoa, whoa, take it easy, kid. I am a good friend of your mother."

Spaz suddenly remembered the car from when Sticky had dropped his mother off a few weeks prior. Spaz signaled his men to put away their weapons and yelled to the car, "What the hell do you want with me?"

Sticky felt the power of Spaz and was impressed. "Hey, kid, come on over and take this ride with me. We need to talk."

"Why would I do that? I don't know you like that."

Sticky smiled. "Listen, kid, I'm a good friend of your mother's, and I need to have a few words with you. It's important."

Spaz looked around at his men. "I'll be right back. Grams, take this ride with me," he demanded as his number one head buster got into the backseat. Whenever anyone mentioned his mother, Spaz was willing to listen. Spaz got seated in the back.

Nikki Montagna sat on the passenger side. Sticky signaled his driver to pull off as they cruised through the raggedy streets of North Philadelphia. Sticky lit up a Cuban cigar and began to speak. "Let's talk, kid. Your mother is going through a difficult time, and I'm here to help. Here, have a cigar and some champagne."

"Never smoked one of these before. I smoke strictly weed." Spaz lit up the cigar filled with cannabis.

"Okay, kid. I see you are independent, and I like that. You know that will take you a long way in this cold world."

Spaz blew the weed smoke out of his nose, letting the words from Sticky soak in. He noticed his accent, fancy suits, jewelry and a gun bulging out of Nikki's suit jacket. *Oh shit*! he thought. "This motherfucker just might be Mafia related," he mumbled to Grams.

Sticky blew smoke out his mouth from the Cuban cigar. A diamond ring decorated his pinky.

"So, what did you want to talk to me about?" Spaz stared around the car.

"Listen, kid, call me Sticky."

Spaz stared out the window.

"To answer your question, I wanted to talk to you about the trouble you have been getting into."

"So, you pick me up to lecture me? I don't need that right now."

Nikki stared at Sticky with disagreement written on his face.

"Do I look like an individual who gives lectures? I give orders, kid."

"You goddamn right," said Nikki.

The Italian accent and aggressive delivery reminded Spaz of a Mafia movie. "Listen, Sticky, the Black Boss Family is a gang that I run. We got these streets on lock. People pay me ten thousand dollars a month to breathe around this motherfucker. My niggas a die for me, and guess what, Sticky? I will die for them too."

Grams nodded in agreement.

Sticky was moved by the kid's loyalty. "Spaz, you speak with truth, courage, and great leadership. How can I tell you to leave your organization alone when I am in the same type of family? But my family is wealthier and more powerful. The game is the same. The Scilionni family truly runs the city, kid."

Spaz's eyes lit up. He recalled many legendary stories about the Scilionni family, from drugs, extortion, racketeering, gambling, murder, and mayhem across the city of Philadelphia. Spaz took a deep breath and puffed on his cigar.

"So, kid, the bottom line is that I am a good friend of your mother's, and she is worried about your whereabouts. I do not want to make you do anything, but I am going to offer my assistance to get you out of this hood and into a mansion if you like. In addition to that, I will introduce you to a lifestyle that offers luxury cars, yachts, entrepreneurship, and more. I will supply you with ammunition to get rid of your enemies. By working with me, you will never have to get your hands dirty," Sticky said, looking at Spaz like a dollar sign.

Spaz's eyes became bloodshot red as he received the offer of a lifetime. "You have got to be shittin' me, right? Who do I have to kill?"

Sticky and Nikki Montagna began to laugh.

"Cool it, kid. Do you know anything about cocaine?"

"Of course I do. My man Reel left me his empire that supplied a major load to the city. He got locked up recently, and now I am in search of a new supplier."

Sticky blew smoke from his mouth. "How quick you can move a kilo?"

"I just sold two keys this month. I got motel buildings full of fiends," said Spaz.

"I got birds for thirty-five. That's cheap with this drought going on," Sticky said.

Reel taught me always get the best price. "I got thirty."

This nigger thinks he smart. "Thirty-two and I'll give you another kilo on consignment."

I can work with that. "We got a deal"

"Okay then, you keep your head screwed on straight and you're going to go far in this business." *I'm supposed to be helping the kid, not get him into more trouble. Oh well, fuck it. If he's gonna buy drugs I'd rather it be from me.*

The sky grew dark and Sticky's Jaguar pulled back in front of the Black Boss Family's headquarters.

"Here, kid, take my number and give me a call this coming Thursday. Oh yeah, kid, if you maintain a good business relationship, you will be a multimillionaire," he said with laughter. "But on the other hand, if you fuck this money up, you might not make it."

Spaz laughed sarcastically. "No worries. I count my money down to the penny. I have every intention of becoming a multimillionaire. You're not issuing threats already, are you?"

"I don't issue threats, kid . . . Thursday."

Spaz and Grams exited the car carrying bags. The car sped up the block as Spaz and Grams headed into BBF headquarters.

"That Mafia fool said he don't issue threats," Grams told Spaz. "Don't he know I'll shoot him in the top of his head for talking like that to you."

"Let's hope he never has to find that out," Spaz said, patting Grams on the back.

Chapter Thirteen
ATTRACTION OF A SAVAGE

"Yo, chill. Listen to this article I'm reading in the newspaper," said Cola, who was the ringleader of the female BBF. She used to be Chips' main squeeze. It was her loud mouth that Spaz heard talking about how Chips was double crossing Reel. After his death, Spaz kept her close to him and after leading the leader of a rival gang into an ambush while Grams filled his body with bullets, Cola was initiated into the Black Boss Family. Over the years, she grew over confident, arrogant, seductive, and extremely dangerous. She also grew an oversized backside that was shaped like a Valentine's Day heart.

"Listen to this," said Cola. "Massacre in the Badlands leaves ten dead and three others wounded in a shootout yesterday in North Philadelphia. Officers responding to reports of gunfire found the victims about six in the evening." Cola closed the newspaper.

"Yo, who the fuck is that pulling up?" Princess asked, observing a Toyota Camry with dents on the passenger door. Princess was slim, light-skinned, and sassy, but also Cola's partner in crime. She joined BBF by stabbing a rival over an unpaid debt to Reel.

"Oh, that's my little cousin, Martini," Cola responded.

"Well, damn, what that bitch was in? A car wreck? The side of her whip is fucked up," Princess said, receiving laughter from her comment.

"What is she doing? Moving in with you?" she asked, observing Martini getting out the car carrying a few gym bags.

Cola frowned. "Hell no!"

Martini headed toward the front door. "Hey, cousin."

"Don't 'hey cousin' me. Where do you think you're going with all those bags?"

"Grandma didn't tell you I got kicked out my house? Long story."

"No she didn't tell me you was moving in, and I got time, so start explaining," Cola said, folding up her newspaper.

Martini had a pretty, honey brown complexion, with a body like a favorite porno star. "I don't feel like explaining," said Martini with an attitude. She tried to make her entrance but was blocked by Cola and her crew.

"You're not going anywhere until you tell me what's going on. I call shots around here. Not Grandma." Cola was dead serious.

Martini felt defeated, rolling her eyes behind the shades of her Christian Dior designer frames. "Look, my boyfriend of five years found out that I had been lying to him about my occupation." Martini twisted her lips, holding back her tears.

"What? What's your occupation? I barely see you. I don't know what you got going on," said Cola, noticing how thick and in shape Martini appeared. *She looking good as hell. If she wasn't my cousin, ooh . . .*

Tears started rolling down Martini's eyes. "I didn't know he was going to act the way he acted. He didn't have to hit me," she cried.

"Hold up. Slow down . . . he hit you?" Cola barked. "Damn, bitch, what kind of job you got that a make a nigga hit you?" Cola said, looking her cousin up and down. "Oh shit you a stripper!"

"Yeah, I dance. I needed the money. His broke ass can't take care of me. I need a real man."

"Man, fuck that! That nigga hit you?" asked Cola. "Is that why you wearing them damn glasses?" She snatched Martini's glasses off her face.

"Aww hell naw!" Cola said when she saw how damaged Martini's right eye was. "Yo shit black, swollen, and closed shut. Oh, fuck that! Ain't *nobody* going to be putting they hands on my family."

"Damn! You got knocked the fuck out!" Princess joked.

"Fuck y'all," said Martini.

Cola got on the phone and dialed a number. It rang twice before she got an answer.

"What your crazy ass want?" said Grams.

"Yo, Grams, where y'all at?"

"We at the headquarters playing pool. Why? What's up?"

"Okay, I need to holler at you. It's an emergency. I'm on my way!" Cola hung up the phone. "Come on, y'all. We gone get to the bottom of this shit!"

Martini dropped her bags in the living room.

"Come on, bitch. You coming with me. So come on and start up this raggedy-ass piece-of-shit car you got," Cola demanded.

The BBF headquarters stood on the corner of Twentieth Street. The sign read: BBF Rim-Shop. But the inside told a different story.

An elderly man in a suit answered the door. "Good evening, ladies. How could I help you?"

Cola grew angry. "Kevin, if you don't get ya crack head ass out my way." She barged through the living room with a tight grip on Martini's hand.

Nude young ladies sat at a huge dinner table packaging drugs. Martini couldn't believe her eyes walking through the kitchen and down into the basement.

Spaz, Grams, and Slugger stood over the pool table with piles of money on the edge.

"Bet a stack that I hit this red ball in the corner pocket," Spaz said with confidence.

"Okay, it's a bet." Slugger pushed his money up.

"Me too. You're not hitting that muthafucka in, player," Grams said.

"I'm a show y'all muthafuckas something," Spaz said, aiming his stick and slowly pushing it in and out of a circular hole he made with his finger. "This is how I fuck my queens, nice and slow!" he yelled while knocking the red ball in the corner pocket. "Money out of sight starts a fight. Get mines or get naked," he boasted while counting the money he won.

Cola barged into the basement interrupting their gambling. "Look what this bitch-ass nigga did to my cousin!" said Cola in a rage.

"Damn, that's crazy!" Grams said, observing her wounds.

"Who did that to you?" Slugger said.

"You all right?" Spaz asked, with strong eye contact.

At that moment the world froze. Martini felt Spaz's familiar presence. *There's something about his eyes.*

"Do I know you from somewhere?" Spaz asked. "Even with a bruised eye, you're still beautiful." He slid his finger down her hairline.

"Thank you, and you look familiar also."

"Niggaz like beating up on girls? Okay, I'ma take care of this one personally."

Ronny was a good kid who didn't get in any trouble on the streets. He and Martini's birthday were two days apart. They both were twenty-one. He stood six feet tall. Everybody always said that Ronny looked just like Chris Brown. Ronny was at the corner store on Sixty-eighth and Ogontz drinking a bottle of Gatorade, thinking of his future as an NBA basketball player. Ronny was a senior at Duke University and was ready to live out his basketball dream. But with love on his mind, he couldn't focus. He couldn't think straight or get Martini off his mind. He never dreamed that she would earn a living dancing in a strip club, and it instantly broke his heart. He slammed his beverage to the ground and walked to his grandmother's house.

Four SUVs parked in front of him. He prayed it wasn't the police for domestic abuse. He continued walking toward his grandmother's house. As he walked past the tinted SUV, the window rolled down.

Who the hell is that? Ronny kept walking and picked up the pace.

"Yo, Ronny? Come here for a second," said Spaz.

"Who, me?" Ronny asked, seeing the gangster sitting behind the wheel. Fear entered his gut. *Shit! Who is this dude?*

"Yeah, you. Come over here." Spaz put his serious face on. He was dressed in all black, including the tight leather gloves on his hands.

Ronny walked toward the SUV. "What's up, man?" he asked, noticing Martini in the front seat. He glanced at Spaz. "Hey, what's up?"

Spaz smiled devilishly. "I know you're wondering who I am. My name is Spaz, but you can call me the love counselor. Get in."

"I can't get in. My grandmother is expecting me," he said nervously.

"This only going to take a minute. If you think about running, I got goons parked up and down this block ready for my signal to lay your ass down. Now, we can do this the hard way or the easy way. You can get your ass shot right now, or you can get in and talk to me." Spaz waited, impatient for Ronny to respond.

Ronny made a wise decision and climbed into the car. Grams and Slugger sat in the backseat.

"Yo, lift ya fucking arms up, nigga!" Grams demanded.

"Please don't kill me. I didn't do anything," Ronny responded, lifting his arms as they requested.

"Shut the fuck up, pussy!" said Grams, searching Ronny for weapons.

"I'm not carrying any weapons," cried Ronny.

"Is he clean?" asked Spaz.

"Yeah, his bitch ass ain't strapped," said Grams as Spaz drove through the intersection.

Petrified, Ronny stared out the window. "Where we going?" he asked.

"For a little ride. Is there anything you want to say to this young lady?" said Spaz, referring to Martini.

Ronny glanced at the back of Martini's head, and then at the entourage of SUVs trailing behind.

"Aww man." Ronny began to cry. "What you gone do to me, man?" he asked. "Come on, man. I'm about to go to the NBA. I ain't with all the drama."

Martini began to cry.

"I'm sorry I put my hands on you," said Ronny.

"Look what you did to my face!" Martini screamed. She took off her shades, turned back to look at him, exposing her damaged right eye.

Spaz grew angrier seeing the bruise. He pressed his foot on the gas, eager to get to his destination quicker.

"I'm sorry, baby. You know I didn't mean it." Ronny had regret written on his face.

"She is not trying to hear that sorry shit, nigga!" Spaz said furiously. "Do you know who she is to me?"

Ronny's lips began to shiver. "Your cousin?"

"Naw!"

"Your niece or half-sister?"

"Wrong again!" Spaz arrived in the Uptown section of Philadelphia. He reached BBF member, Big Bob's body shop.

Two SUVs slowed down in front of the body shop. The garage door opened and Spaz and his crew drove inside. Then the sound of car doors slamming emerged as the BBF exited their vehicles.

"Since you can't figure out who she is to me then let me tell you. This is my new girl, muthafucka!" Spaz smacked Ronny in the head with his fist and exited the driver side.

Ronny's door flew open. "No, please!"

Spaz grabbed him and snatched him out the backseat and slammed him up against the wall. "You like hitting girls, nigga?"

"No, I don't. She was lying to me, man. She's a stripper!" he cried, catching blows to his ribs. "Huuuuuh!" Ronny felt the impact of his bones cracking. "Uuugghh!" Two hard punches to the face knocked blood out of his mouth.

The BBF gathered around to watch the violent activities.

"Fuck that nigga up!" Cola said, walking toward Ronny. "Hold up!!" She kicked him in the testicles and watched him fall to the ground.

"Stop! Man, don't do this!" Ronny begged.

"Hold that nigga up!" Spaz said.

"With pleasure," Slugger said, putting Ronny in a wrestling headlock while Grams held his legs. "Fuck him up!" Slugger said, after getting a tight grip on Ronny.

Martini watched as Ronny got beat down. She began to feel guilty. *They're going to kill him.* "Stop! He's had enough," Martini finally said.

Spaz ignored Martini's statement and punched him with hard combinations of jabs and hooks. And for the next five minutes he used Ronny for a human punching bag. "You like hitting girls?" asked Spaz.

"No, please!" Ronny whispered with no energy to talk.

Slugger slammed Ronny to the ground. He landed on his face, knocking one of his teeth loose. "Bitch-ass nigga."

Ronny was unconscious and bleeding badly with a swollen face. "Now you see how it feel, muthafucka!" Cola yelled, kicking Ronny in the ribs.

Spaz was out of breath from beating up Ronny. His leather gloves were covered in blood. "Ay, yo, Slugger, drive that nigga to the hospital and say you saw him bleeding on the road and dropped his ass off. If we leave him here, he is going to die."

"All right, I got you," Slugger said. "Help me get this tall, basketball-playing ass nigga in the car." Grams and Slugger carried Ronny to the car and tossed him in the backseat.

Martini was in tears. She hurt worse, watching him get his ass beat than him beating her ass.

Cola hugged her. "You okay, cuz'? Come on, we outta here," said Cola, wiping the tears from Martini's eyes. "Go 'head and get back in the car with Spaz. He must really like your ass for him to be going all out for you."

"Come on, ma," Spaz said to Martini while waiting by his truck.

"Go ahead, girl. I'm riding with Slugger to drop this nigga off at the hospital," Cola said.

"Is he going to be okay?" she asked, walking toward Spaz.

Spaz held the door open for her as she climbed inside.

"He will be all right. But fuck that nigga-bitch. He just blacked your eye."

The garage door opened and the entourage of SUVs exited the body shop.

Martini replayed the beat down in her head. "Thank you for what you did," she said in tears.

"That was fun. *Thank you.*" Spaz noticed the pain in her aura. "You okay? I'm sorry if I got carried away. I don't like niggaz that beat on females."

"Did you really mean what you said in the car?"

"About what, sweetheart?" he asked, turning up Broad Street.

"About me being your new girl?" said Martini.

"I don't know. What do you think?"

"I think you were serious. I mean, I hope you were serious." She smiled. "It's something about you."

Spaz stopped at a red light and kissed her lips and tasted her tongue.

"You with me now. You know what that means?" he asked.

"Uh, can you please inform me?" She smiled, waiting for the light to turn green.

"It means you're my girl, so there will be no lying, no stealing, and no cheating. Keep it real with me because I take loyalty very, very serious."

Martini noticed Spaz's somber disposition. "I respect you and I'm loyal. I want to be with you. You're my hero." *And you're fine and paid!*

The two shared an intimate kiss as Martini stared into Spaz's eyes. *I know this nigga from somewhere.*

Chapter Fourteen
CITY OF BROTHERLY SLUGS

A year had passed and Spaz smiled at his dad, Flash, who had just stepped out of Fairton Federal Correctional Facility a free man after ten long years of being trapped in the belly of the beast. Now Flash was rescued by time. He smiled as he heard the sounds of music blasting and saw his son behind the steering wheel of a black Lincoln Navigator.

"Heyyy, what's up, baby boy!" he said as Spaz got out the SUV. The two hugged immediately. *This nigga's almost bigger than me now.*

"Come on, Dad. Let's get out of this dump," Spaz said, getting back behind the steering wheel. Flash got in the passenger side and Spaz drove into the intersection.

"Man, you out here driving fancy SUVs and dressed in the latest fashions. What the fuck? You didn't listen to nothing I told you, huh? Did you read my letters at all?"

Spaz felt his brows narrowing out of irritation, but didn't want to ruin the happy moment. He took a deep breath. "Of course I read them, Dad."

Flash stared at his freedom through the windshield. "I'm home, baby!"

"How does it feel?"

"Damn good . . . real good. But back to you and this BBF business."

Spaz sat up straight in his seat. "Come on, Dad. Let's just enjoy our time together," said Spaz, stealing a quick glance at Flash.

"Yeah, okay 'enjoy our time together'. You something else, all grown up."

"Why you sweating me, man? I know what you need" Spaz drove a few miles and exited the highway.

Twenty minutes later, Spaz parked out front of the restaurant. "Come on, Pops," said Spaz, exiting the truck.

"Oh snap! Super Steaks! I haven't had a cheese steak in ten years!" said Flash.

Spaz sat behind the steering wheel with the car in park. He reached in the backseat and placed a gym bag on Flash's lap. "That's for you."

"What the fuck is this?" Flash opened the bag and paused. He pulled out a bulletproof vest and a Glock 40.

"Listen, Pop, shit is real out here. These niggas in the city is like wild barbarians. Niggas getting kilt every day.

"Man, I don't need this."

"A lot has changed since ten years ago. I did a lot of dirt out here and you never know."

"This my first day out of jail, and you hand me a vest and a strap!"

"Just put it on. Better to be safe than sorry," he said, stepping out of the truck.

Flash remained seated with the vest in his hand. "My own son, giving me a vest and a gun," he mumbled. Flash thought about all the senseless shootings that he used to read about in the Philadelphia newspaper when he was in prison. "Fuck it." He took his sweat shirt off and slid on the bulletproof vest. Then he put his sweatshirt back on. "I haven't worn one of these in a while," said Flash, placing the gun on his waist. "Wait for me, young b'oy."

Spaz and Flash walked into the restaurant. "How tall is you now, boy?"

"I'm five-eleven," said Spaz.

"Damn, you almost taller than me."

They walked up to the counter and stood in front of the cashier. "Hey, can I get two cheese steaks, please?"

"Sure, would that be all, sir?" said the cashier.

"And two pineapple sodas."

"Okay, your total is $18.99."

"Yes ma'am."

"Look at you, ova here ballin' like a muthafucka," said Flash, staring at the knot of bills Spaz pulled out of his pocket.

After the steaks were cooked and packaged, Spaz and Flash walked back to the truck. They drove up the Valley Forge Highway. They conversed about life and how he wanted Spaz to stay out the streets, but every time he brought up the subject, Spaz would talk about something different.

They exited City Line Avenue and drove through a few lights until they arrived in front of an attractive three-bedroom house. Spaz parked the truck.

"Come on, Pops. I got to show you something," he said, heading toward the front door.

Where the hell is he taking me? "Wait for me, son," said Flash, walking behind him. Inside, the house was fully furnished. New carpet, nice paintings, and a huge flat screen decorated the living room.

"Follow me," Spaz said, heading up the stairway.

Spaz ignored his statement and walked to the master bedroom. "There's nothing illegal in this house."

"Whose house is this?" asked Flash.

"It's yours," said Spaz, handing Flash a set of keys from his pocket.

"What, son?" Flash wore a surprised expression.

"This is your house," he said, handing him the keys.

A huge smile of appreciation decorated Flash's mouth. *I can't let him see me cry.* "Yo, man, I can't explain the feeling that I have flowing through my body. Thank you for believing in me. Thank you for the money orders and letters and now this. Thanks, son." Flash hugged Spaz tight as if it would be his last time seeing him. "Okay, enough with this sentimental shit. I know you grown now, and you think you a gangster, but you always going to be my little boy. You hear me?"

"Yeah, Dad. I love you, man," Spaz said, returning a hug. A tear dropped from his eye. "I got some business to take care of. If you need me call me." Spaz broke their embrace. He wasn't used to having the type of emotions he was feeling. His lifestyle didn't allow for it.

"Oh, okay, all right, solid. Well, you just be careful. I need you out here. I need you to survive the game. Everybody don't live long enough to retire."

"I hear you, Dad. We gone talk more later, okay?"

"All right, son."

Flash watched from the hallway as Spaz headed out the front door. *They grow up so fast.* "Yess! I got a house! Whooo!" said Flash while running downstairs to lock the front door. He toured the house and counted his blessings. "This shit is dope." he said, admiring the home.

Flash walked back upstairs and opened the master bedroom. He glanced around at the huge room. *Holy shit!* "Baby, is that you?" he said to the gorgeous woman lying in his bed. She was freshly bathed and smelled like Tommy Girl lotion and perfume. Her long blonde hair was wrapped in a ponytail, and she was wearing see through lingerie from Victoria Secret.

"Welcome home, Flash," said Pearl.

Spaz pulled up at Tops-Up Lounge in South Philly. He headed inside and walked straight to the back. Only a few customers occupied the bar. Tuesdays were always slow.

Spaz was greeted by Sticky in his office. "Come on in, kid," said Sticky, smoking on a Cuban cigar.

Spaz placed a bag of money on Sticky's desk.

"Heyy, good week, hunh?" Sticky laughed and pinched Spaz's cheek. "What I tell you? Didn't I tell you, you would be rich? Hunh?" Sticky puffed his cigar and took a seat. "What's wrong, kid? You just made your first million dollars. What's the sad face for?"

Spaz took a seat. "Sticky, I need you to do me a favor?"

"You name him, he's dead!" Sticky laughed.

"No, it's not that."

"Well, what is it?"

"I need you to stop seeing my mother," Spaz said with a serious look on his face.

Sticky grew quit. "Forget about it, don't worry."

"My dad's home," said Spaz.

Sticky's heart dropped. *That's that motherfucker that I let hear me fucking his broad.* "That's good, real good. I'm happy for him. What's the problem?"

"I want them back together with no interruptions. I know how you feel about my mom, but for business sake I need you to stop."

Sticky hesitated. "Sure, kid. That's your mother. I would feel the same as you. I want us to continue doing business together, Spaz. Don't worry. Forget about it," said Sticky. He put his cigar out. "So we should be celebrating. Congratulations! You made your first million dollars. Come 'ere," said Sticky, hugging Spaz to make him feel comfortable, but Spaz remained displeased, feeling the tension in the air.

Chapter Fifteen
MOMMA'S BOY

A news flash interrupted the moment. "This is Tom Arnold reporting live from Twentieth and Brown where a house fire took the lives of Saleem Henchmen and Pearl Gravamina. This incident occurred just hours ago as the fire erupted at 4040 North Twentieth Street."

Spaz's eyes grew wide. He couldn't control the tears that ran down his face. "Fuck!"

One week later ...

The Black Boss Family paid their respects, as well as Sticky and a few members of the Scilionni family. Spaz placed a dozen flowers in his parents' caskets. Tears dropped from his eyes.

Spaz approached Sticky and the two hugged. "My mom and dad are gone."

Sticky stared Spaz in the eyes. "Listen, kid, you will always have a father in me."

"Detectives looked at the surveillance video from the security cameras," said Spaz with pain in his eyes, "and there was no sign of anyone going inside the house."

"I know how you think, kid. Things happen. What do you do?"

"Nothing. Keep getting rich, I guess . . ." All the power and money that Spaz and Sticky possessed couldn't bring his parents back.

Spaz scheduled an emergency meeting two weeks later at Oz strip club. He parked his black S-Class and jumped out looking fresh to death.

Slugger climbed out the passenger side throwing the last bit of the Dutch filled with hydro to the street. "Yo, it's time to grab some ass!"

Grams exited the back holding a bottle of Patron. "That's what the fuck I am talking about!"

The three gangsters entered the club. The sound of cheering customers enjoying the strippers and loud music blasting through the speakers was nostalgic. Topless dancers were sliding up and down the poles. Spaz walked toward the VIP section where they were greeted with a bottle of Rosé by the hostess.

Spaz took a deep breath as he turned toward Grams and Slugger. "I'm sure you know why I called this meeting. The gang wars are now history! All the fallen soldiers, rest in peace. Now we are fighting a different war. The drug war! This crack shit has changed history. Most of the old gangsters are strung out on this shit or selling it. Now we have the strongest drug clique around this motherfucker. We are making one hundred thousand dollars a week! There are hustlers out here making more than us, but the only difference is they are weak! These enemies, our so-called competition, are soft. Even though we are getting money, we have to stay hungry. Now with a connection like Sticky supplying us with bricks and all the guns we need, we can't go wrong. Now, our biggest assets are the motels. That's a fucking crack fiend's gold mine! I heard nut-ass niggas been intercepting our traffic. Now, I already warned them niggas, and I'm done talking."

Grams eyes grew bloodshot red. "You already know what it is. I will bury them fucking clowns! They don't want it. They got the game fucked up, cousin." Grams was up to thirteen murders and he enjoyed it.

Slugger was both killer and hustler. "Spaz. Grams and I will handle it. Don't worry, we got this."

Spaz nodded his head. "That's what the fuck I'm talking about. I want you and Grams to take care of these ignorant motherfuckers."

The three shook hands, enjoyed a few lap dances and headed toward the exit, followed by the prettiest strippers in the club.

"So you want us to follow you to the hotel?" asked the leader of the female crew.

"Hell yeah. Don't get lost, baby," said Spaz with lust in his eyes.

"Okay, we know the way. We will meet y'all there," she said, blowing Spaz a kiss, then switching her hips side to side on her way to her car.

Slugger grabbed his private. "Man, I got a take a leak."

Grams agreed. "Me too."

Spaz smiled. "Damn, I see you gangsters had too many bottles of Rosé. I'll be waiting in the car."

Spaz headed out the club door into the night air of the Philly streets. He strolled through the parking lot and rested in his S-Class. He thought about the success he had been having and about the death of his mom and dad.

His thoughts were broken up by the two stickup boys who had opened his door. Both were wearing baseball caps tilted over their eyes, making it hard to identify their faces. Both stickup boys pointed pistols in his face.

Spaz stared death in the eyes. It was either give up the money or get shot. "You got it, fam'. Take what you want."

One of the stickup boys reached in Spaz's pocket, damn near ripping his pockets off. "Give me this shit, bitch!"

The other stickup kid quickly pushed the bankroll in his pockets while steadily aiming his .357 in Spaz's face. Then he violently snatched Spaz's chain from his neck. "Take that fucking Rolex off, nigga!"

Slugger zipped his pants up and stepped from behind the dumpster. His eyes were a little blurry from the liquor he had been drinking, but he was able to see the two gunmen running away from the S-Class that Spaz was sitting in. "What the fuck!" Slugger pulled out his Glock-40 and ran toward the car. "Yo, Grams, come on, fam'!"

Grams came from behind the dumpster, still pulling up his zipper. "What the fuck is going on?"

Spaz was furious. He reached under his seat for his .45. "Yo, I just got robbed!"

Slugger and Grams hopped in the car as Spaz pulled off in the same direction as the two stickup boys.

The stickup boys ran fast around the corner. They were out of breath but made it to their getaway car, which was parked on a dark and narrow street.

"Yo, I'm tired as shit. Hurry up and open up the door!" one of the stickup kids said.

"I am," he replied, reaching inside his pocket and pulling out the car keys. The money from the robbery fell to the street. "Oh shit!" he yelled.

"Fuck is you doing?"

"I dropped the fuckin' money!" he said, scooping the cash off the ground and stuffing it back in his pocket. They hopped inside of a raggedy Cadillac.

"You get it all?" the other one said after climbing into the passenger side.

"Yeah, nigga, we out of here!" he said, getting seated behind the steering wheel.

He put the key in the ignition, but before he could put the car in gear, a loud gunshot went off and a bullet came crashing through the driver's side window. Hollow points exploded inside the driver's head. Blood painted the windshield. The passenger screamed in fear as he saw chunks of brain, blood, and skull fragments on his lap. He took deep breaths, on the verge of going into shock from the gunshots and seeing his friend's head explode in front of him.

He saw Grams looking down on him from the driver's side with the devil in his eyes. The passenger tried to make a run for it, but Slugger pressed an automatic weapon against his temple.

"Yo, get the fuck back in the car, pussy!"

Against his will he sat back in the car and began contemplating his death.

"Yo, get my nigga his fucking chain back and his money!" His hand shivered as he reached into his dead friend's pockets and grabbed the bankroll.

Slugger snatched the money out of his hands. "Now get him his chain back, you nut-ass nigga!"

The terrified robber grabbed the blood-soaked chain from his friend's bloody neck, trying not to vomit as he offered it back to Slugger, who grabbed the chain and glanced at Grams. Grams and Slugger took a deep breath and began firing shots. Fifteen hollow point slugs ate through his flesh. His body jerked back and forth as he died.

Grams smiled. "I bet you won't be robbing anybody else, motherfucka."

Spaz drove to the scene of the crime. "Yo, hurry up!"

Slugger and Grams ran back to the whip and hopped in. Spaz pulled off with the tires burning rubber.

Five minutes later, Spaz exited the highway.

"That was Maine setting us up to get robbed," said Slugger.

"How do you know, nigga?" said Grams.

"Because I recognized the driver. That was Little Rick."

"Little Rick? Maine's young cousin?" asked Spaz.

"Yeah, that nigga knew who you was. I bet you Maine put him up to it," said Grams.

"Yo, do some research on that before we make a move on Maine," said Spaz.

"Say no more."

"This bitch ass nigga killed my cousin," said Maine, staring down at Little Rick while lying in his casket. The funeral wasn't that crowded and the spring day sent chills up Maine spine. His finger itched from the lust of revenge.

Spaz walked inside the church accompanied by Grams and Slugger. Spaz walked to the viewing of Little Rick's body and stood by Maine. "The next time you send your folks to rob me you going to be next to lay in one of these coffins," said Spaz.

Maine lost his cool and grabbed Spaz and swung a wild right hook. Spaz dodged the punch and pushed Maine a few steps back. Grams and Slugger stepped in front of Spaz and cocked back their guns.

"Nigga, you in violation!" said Grams.

"There's a time and place for everything," said Spaz, placing his Cartier glasses on. "Let's go," he demanded, heading out of the church.

"You know I always wanted to slide up inside of you, girl," said Spaz.

"What about Martini? You know that's my best friend Cola's cousin," said Princess.

"What she don't know won't hurt her." He smiled and kissed her neck.

"Ohh, that feels good," she said, getting into the moment. Princess turned and pulled his love muscle out his pants and began sucking.

"Yeah, just like that," he said, enjoying the sensation.

"You must feel like a king," she said, then continued slurping away on his dick.

"What makes you say that?" Spaz asked, watching her head go up and down.

"You have women throwing they self to you like you royalty," she replied, then finished slurping.

"It does feel good, but . . ."

"But what," she asked, gulping faster.

"Ahhh!" Spaz busted a nut. Princess swallowed every drop.

"Damn, you got some powerful head," said Spaz, walking to the bathroom. He turned the shower on and adjusted the temperature to hot.

Princess stripped naked and lay under the covers, hoping Spaz would return and lay his pipe deep into her soul.

Spaz washed a day's worth of dirt off his body and dried off.

"Pop! Pop! Pop!" were the sounds that he heard coming from the bedroom.

"What the fuck!" He grabbed his spare gun from under the bathroom sink and headed toward the bedroom. He peeked around the corner of the hallway with the barrel of his gun leading the way. Spaz entered the bedroom. "Princess?" he called but received no reply. He moved in closer. "Princess?" he said again, noticing her body under the covers. A feather floated from the ceiling down to the floor.

The sound of tires screeching made Spaz run to the window. He looked out and saw a black Impala speeding up the block. "Damn!" He walked to the bed and pulled the covers back. "Oh no!" Princess lay in bed with a pillow over her head. He moved the pillow and saw her brains oozing out of her head and onto the bed.

"Mutherfucka!"

"Ay man, this Spaz. I called you from a throw away phone," he told Reel, who was walking the yard and picked up the call the moment he felt the phone vibrate.

"Okay, because I didn't notice the number."

"Listen, man, ya boy Mizane is a done dizeal," said Spaz, speaking in code about murdering Maine.

"What happened?" Reel asked.

Spaz continued to speak in code. "He out here tryna take me izout so he can be the next kizing. Lives got lizost and it got to be done."

"I knew he was going to be a problem. Do what you got to do. Just keep it quiziet," Reel said and ended the call.

"Y'all niggas sit right here and direct all these crack heads to come to our trap spot on Cambridge Street," said Maine, observing crack heads walking toward the motels.

"I got you, big homie," said Storm.

"I'm a holla at y'all niggas later," Maine said, hopping in his four door coupe turbo charged Mercedes-Benz. "Hit my phone, nigga," he said, driving off.

Maine knew that directing drug traffic toward his establishment would cause problems with Spaz. Spaz had already sent a message to Maine to take his business elsewhere.

"Yo! Yo! Yo! Where are you going? We got that real butter shit right here," Storm said to crack head Kevin, who was a loyal customer to Spaz. Three goons were protecting Storm.

"Yo, I'm cool. I want the black bags," replied the crack head.

Storm snapped. "Fuck that Spaz shit. Our shit is better than those black bags."

Crack head Kevin yelled back, "The black bags are the best in the city. You got to step your game up."

Storm frowned. "What, nigga? I'll slap you in your ugly-ass face."

Storm's goons noticed the commotion. "Yo, knock that stupid motherfucker out, Storm!" said one of his goons.

Storm took his's advice and punched crack head Kevin in the face, knocking him out cold. Storm stood over Kevin and took his money out of his pocket. "Give me this shit, bitch!"

Slugger and Grams were parked across the street from where Storm and his crew were hustling. "Peep that. There they go right there. Maine got the nerve to be sending these niggas out here to hustle on our block."

Grams cocked his Desert Eagle back and got out the car as Slugger slid out the driver seat.

Storm saw Grams coming and grew nervous. "Yo, y'all got the straps?"

"Yeah, they in the stash. Why?"

"'Cause here come Grams and them."

"Oh shit!" the thug said and took off running. The other two goons stood by Storm.

Grams approached Storm. "Yo, didn't we tell y'all not to hustle around here no more?" Grams aimed at Storm's head and squeezed the trigger.

Blouw!

One shot blew the top of Storm's head off.

The two gangsters tried to run for their guns, but hollow point slugs in their backs slammed their bodies to the ground.

Grams walked over top of Storm's body. "Learn how to respect the boss, bitch!" He unloaded the clip into his dead body.

Slugger ran over to Grams. "Yo, this motherfucker is already dead! Come on, we out!"

Slugger and Grams ran back to the Dodge Charger and opened the doors and jumped in. Slugger pulled off, upset with Grams. "Yo, man, what is wrong with you?"

"What the fuck you mean 'what's wrong with me'. Don't you ever stop me when I'm giving a nigga a closed casket!" Grams responded.

Slugger shook his head. "You trippin'!" He didn't need to see Grams in action again to understand that Grams was a cold-blooded killer.

Chapter Sixteen
FEMALE KING

"So why was that bitch dead in your bed, Spaz?" asked Martini.

"First of all, I told you stop talking on this phone like that. And second of all, Slugger used my room. She wasn't with me," he said, hanging up on Martini.

"'Cause I'm rich, bitch!" said Spaz, smiling and repeating the famous words of Dave Chappelle.

Slugger and Grams burst out laughing as they all sat in the same office where Reel used to sit.

"Yo, who is on our level? This nigga Maine hating because we got North Philly on smash! Nobody can fuck with us."

Slugger rubbed his chin. "Ay yo, Spaz, it's this boy named Redz from out west. He eating like crazy. He robs banks, sells bricks, and he got this bad bitch. Her name is Tamika, but everybody call her Stilletto because she be wearing all the new stilettos before they touch the stores. Shorty fly as shit. This bitch is bad. I am talking about long pretty hair, cute-ass face, titties like blouw! Ass like boom! She helps Redz with his drug business. She doesn't ask where he is or what time he is coming home—and she a cold killa, sexy, super model bitch. That's why he so successful because he has a strong backbone in his corner."

Spaz said, "Last bitch I was with got a bullet in the dome, but this bitch you talking about—I'm a have to snatch her up."

Slugger shook his head. "She is loyal to Redz. It's going be hard to get to her."

"That is not a difficult task for a boss. Time is the only factor. Let's go find my new queen."

It was no coincidence that Spaz and Slugger cruised up the West Philly neighborhood and spotted Stiletto and her cousin, Teesha on Fifty-sixth and Hobart Street. Slugger licked his lips. "Yo, Spaz, there she is right there."

Spaz spotted Stiletto and was mesmerized by her beauty. "Damn, she nice!" Spaz pulled over and hopped out of his whip. He wore a striped Polo shirt and True Religion jeans. He walked toward the two lovely ladies. Teesha slid her long tongue up and down on the ice cream, as she saw the two handsome men walking toward them.

"Damn, girl, you're getting real freaky with that ice cream," Slugger flirted. "What's your name, ma?"

She smiled from ear to ear. "Teesha."

Stiletto sat on the steps with an attitude. Spaz laid his game down.

"What up, gorgeous?"

Stiletto looked in different directions, acting as if she didn't hear Spaz.

"Damn, mami, why you acting all stuck-up and shit?" Spaz pulled out his bankroll. "You see this? I never sweat a chick, but you might lose out on a good life. I'll tell you what: when you want a real man that knows how to treat a lady . . . or better than that, when you get your mind right, holla at me." Spaz started walking toward his car. "Come on, Slugger, we out."

Slugger had just finished saving Teesha's number into his phone. "Yo, I'll call you later, sexy."

Teesha slurped on the ice cream. "I'll be waiting."

Spaz and Slugger hopped back into the whip.

"Did you get her number?"

Spaz frowned. "Man, fuck that bitch!"

"I told you she wasn't going to be easy," said Slugger, getting seated behind the steering wheel.

"I could have got her, but I just felt a funny feeling standing in her hood."

"Oh, you scared?"

"What? Never that. I just got a weird feeling."

"Oh okay," Slugger said, making a left turn up Market Street.

"That look like Maine bitch ass," said Spaz.

"Where?" asked Slugger.

"Right there in that Monte Carlo two cars ahead."

"That is his bitch ass," said Slugger.

"Pull up on the side of that nigga," yelled Spaz. He cocked back his .45 with chaos boiling inside.

Slugger trailed behind Maine's car until they reached a red light. Then he pulled up beside Maine. Spaz hung out the window aiming his gun at Maine's head. He held the gun in his hand similar to a sharpshooter.

Maine nodded his head to Young Thug's "Stoner. "

"Blouw! Blouw!"

Shots rang out, shattering Maine's driver side window, barely missing his head by inches.

"Oh sh—" Maine pressed his foot on the gas, speeding through the red light. Slugger followed while Spaz positioned himself out of the window and fired more shots, shattering Maine's back window.

Spaz took his time and aimed at the back of Maine's head while Slugger drove.

"Blouww!"

The bullet smacked Maine in the back of his head and opened a bloody hole in Maine's skull. His car swerved out of control and crashed into a motorcycle.

Maine's dead body flew out of the windshield and landed on the street in front of moving traffic. A Mac truck slammed on its brake. Loud screeching noises emerged. And Maine's body was smashed by the collision.

"Damn! You saw that shit?" said Spaz as Slugger entered the highway.

"Hell yeah!" Slugger answered, but held back the vomit that rose to his throat.

Chapter Seventeen
NOBODY MOVE NOBODY GET HURT

S tiletto stood with her handgun aimed at its target. She wore ear plugs so the gunfire wouldn't affect her hearing. Her facial expression displayed aggressiveness. "Die motherfucker!" She squeezed the trigger and kept a tight finger grip. Gunshots echoed through the shooting range. Long flames exited the barrel. Stiletto's wrist jerked after every shot. The sixteen shots hit its target in the head, chest, and stomach. Stiletto sneered at her achievement. "I'm the fuckin' best," she said as she noticed the bull's-eye on the cardboard target.

Three men exited a car wearing ski masks and holding shotguns and handguns. The three men stormed into Washington Mutual Bank.

"Everybody get the fuck down on the ground!" Redz and two of his goons had innocent bystanders lying on the floor screaming. "Shut the fuck up! Nobody move and nobody will get hurt!"

Two of Redz' goons quickly snatched the money bags from behind the counter. "We got it!"

Redz's eyes grew wide at the sight of the money bags. "All right, let's go!" Redz began backing up while holding his weapon.

Detective Robert Peterson was off duty. He lay down on the floor watching the gunmen as he reached for his weapon. He knew he had to take the bad guys down. This could be his answer to the promotion he desired. Thinking about it made his adrenaline race. Detective Peterson reached for his .38 snub nose strapped in his shoulder holster. He successfully got his weapon in his hand and quickly took aim and fired. Everyone panicked and began screaming.

Redz saw one of his goons holding his chest while falling to the ground. "What the fuck!" Redz' eyes grew bloodshot red.

Detective Peterson let off more shots, catching the other associate in the leg.

"Ahhh, shit, my leg!"

Redz spotted the detective on the ground firing shots and began to let off shots of his own at the officer. Within seconds, Detective Peterson was filled with bullet holes. Blood decorated his body as he lay frozen on the floor. One of Redz' goons lay dead. The other suffered a leg wound.

Redz screamed after seeing his friend lying dead. He grabbed the money bags and helped him to his feet. "Oh shit, you hit?"

Stiletto sat in the getaway car wearing all black clothing and a pair of black sunglasses. She placed a black fitted hat on her head. "Come on, motherfucker, come on!" she mumbled. Stiletto stared out of the rearview mirror at an elderly woman walking slowly to her car. A school bus drove past. Pedestrians crossed the street. She stared down Fairmont Street at the bank. She knew that inside of it was chaos and turmoil. "I wish these niggas hurry up. Come on, come on!" She hit the steering wheel and took a deep breath and relaxed in her seat. Stiletto inhaled and blew the anxiety out of her lungs.

Gunshots fired. "What the—" She paused. "Redz!" She pressed her foot on the gas and drove straight toward the bank's entrance. Stiletto hopped the sidewalk, damn near hitting pedestrians. She saw Redz running out the bank with Tom-Tom's arm over his shoulder. "Shoot that mutherfucka and leave him there!" Stiletto yelled. She reached over to the passenger side door and pushed it open.

Redz opened the backseat and pushed Tom-Tom in.

"Ah!" said Tom-Tom, feeling the effects of his gun wound.

"Oh shit!" yelled Stiletto.

"What?" asked Redz.

"It's the cops!" she said, noticing two white officers driving toward them at full speed.

Redz climbed in the front seat with a half million dollars in a huge gym bag.

Stiletto reached down under the seat and clutched an AK-47. She pushed opened the door and stood out in the street and aimed at the cop car as its driver slammed on his brakes, coming to a complete top. The car landed a few feet in front of her, and the officers reached for their weapons. "I ain't going out like Cleo on *Set it Off!*" She began letting off massive rounds of ammo. Bullet holes tore through the white and blue cop car shattering the windshield. The officers' chest, arms, and faces were hit with rapid gunfire. Flesh tore from their bodies and blood sprayed the vehicle.

Stiletto stopped firing and jumped back into the car and slammed her foot on the gas pedal.

Mark Rizzo jumped out of his vehicle and headed in the bank where Detective Peterson's dead body lay. "These motherfuckers think they can get away with killing a cop!" Federal Agent Rizzo noticed a trail of blood from the bank doorway to the sidewalk. "Hey, guys, get me a DNA test on that blood over there by the entrance."

The bank was filled with federal agents. Yellow tape sealed off the entrance. A crowd of citizens watched from a distance. Action News set up their cameras and soon the reporter began offering details about the robbery.

"We are live from the Washington Mutual Bank located on Sixteenth and Fairmont in North Philadelphia. Three armed men wearing all black with masks barged inside the bank around 3:00 p.m. and demanded everyone to hit the ground. Witnesses say that an undercover detective was being held hostage and was able to kill one of the robbers but was fatally killed during the robbery by one of the gunmen. Witnesses say a lone gunman opened fire on the detective after he shot and wounded the other. Peterson was dead when police arrived, and the other two suspects got away."

The camera man aimed his camera at Federal Agent Mark Rizzo. "We will seek justice and find the men who are responsible for this tragedy." Rizzo also didn't mind stumbling upon the half million dollars the robbers had in their possession.

Stiletto and Redz made love on stacks of money. The whole scenery was like a movie set and Stiletto was Meagan Good. The sound of his phone ringing interfered with their cuddling. Stiletto reached over the dresser and grabbed the phone and handed it to Redz.

"Hello? Yo, what's up, Tom-Tom? Where the fuck you been at, nigga? All right, I will meet you in an hour." Redz hung up the phone. "Baby girl, get dressed. I want you to take this ride with me."

"But this is supposed to be our anniversary."

"It's important, ma-ma."

"You know what? This is ridiculous."

"I got to meet up with Tom-Tom and break him off his half of the money," said Redz, loading up his German-Ruger.

"I don't trust Tom-Tom."

"You never did," said Redz, putting on his vest.

"You should kill that nigga and keep the money. He look like the type that'll snitch on us to save his own ass."

"Just come on, yo."

After a twenty-minute ride, Redz and Stiletto pulled to Broad and Girard.

"Listen, Stiletto, park the car and wait for me right here."

"Okay, baby, be careful."

The two kissed. Redz got out of the car and glanced at Stiletto. He immediately focused his attention on his business and began to stroll toward KFC to meet Tom-Tom. From a distance he saw Tom-Tom sitting at a table inside KFC. He smiled from the thought of keeping Tom-Tom's half of the money. Redz thought about the new house he was going to buy for him and Stiletto. Within seconds, his dream turned into a nightmare as federal agents surrounded him.

"Get down on the ground! Don't move, motherfucker!" the agents yelled.

Redz could not believe his eyes and ears. His heart dropped to his ankles.

"Get the fuck down on the ground. Now!"

Redz dropped to his knees. A hard bash from the butt of Agent Rizzo's Glock-40 knocked him unconscious.

Redz was convicted and sentenced to life in the federal penitentiary. Stiletto was his only support. She was there every step of the way and believed that Redz would get out on an appeal. The high-paid lawyer was going to make sure of that. After thirty months of visits, letters, and money orders, Stiletto found out that Redz got a visit from a female who claimed that he was the father of her five-year-old son. Stiletto paced her home waiting for Redz to call from prison.

Redz was having a hard time adjusting to prison life. He sometimes contemplated suicide, but waiting on his chance for an appeal was the only thing stopping him. The only thing that kept him strong was Stiletto. He decided to give her a call, hoping her voice would brighten his day.

"Hello. Hey, baby," Redz said with a wide grin.

"Don't 'hey baby' me! What's up with this bitch coming on my block today talking shit with this little boy that looks just like you?" He didn't need to see her face to know Stiletto was frowning.

Oh shit! "Baby, I don't know what you are talking about?"

"You know what the fuck I am talking about. S0 you was cheating on me with this bitch the whole five years we've been together?"

"Baby, just calm down for a minute. I slipped up. Please, let's deal with it when I get out."

"No, I am not going to calm down. How could you do this to me after all the visits, letters, and all the love I gave you? This is the thanks I get? You ain't shit! And I am getting my phone number changed, so don't call anymore!"

Redz cursed and slammed the phone down after hearing the dial tone.

Stiletto and Teesha walked inside of Joe's Bar and Grill on City Line Avenue. They ordered lunch, then sat down at a small table to eat.

"That nigga ain't right," said Teesha, staring out the window at the view of the parking lot while sipping her drink. .

Stiletto responded. "I think that nigga Tom-Tom is going to snitch on Redz. I *never* trusted that guy. I told Redz he should've been stop fucking with that clown," said Stiletto, pointing her fork while she expressed her rage. "Tom-Tom can't handle no real shit 'cause he a fake nigga." Her neck jerked with an attitude. "And a real nigga can pretend to be a fake nigga, but a fake nigga can never be real!" said Stiletto.

Two stocky African American men wearing black correctional officer uniforms took their seats at a table behind them..

The moment she overheard one of the men say he'd seen something crazy at Graterford prison, it immediately stole her attention because Redz was serving time there. She wondered if it was a prison riot and if anybody got hurt. Although Stiletto was pissed at Redz, she still cared about his well-being. Stiletto reared her head back and tuned in to their conversation

"Reg, I heard it all and seen it all, working at the C.F.C.F County Jail, but what happened at Graterford?" the officer asked his childhood friend.

"Some kid named Mark Odis hung himself inside his cell. Man, I don't care how many times I've seen it. I can never get over that shit. Sad man . . . just sad . . ."

Stiletto's mouth dropped. "Did he say Mark Odis?" she asked Teesha.

Teesha gasped. "Oh my God! I think he did. Go ask him, Stiletto, just to make sure. Go on, girl!"

Stiletto walked over to the two officers' table and faced the husky guy sitting on her left. "Excuse me, sir. Do you work at Graterford?"

"Yeah, I do," he said, noticing Stiletto's fat ass.

"I don't mean to be eavesdropping, but did you say Mark Odis hung himself?" asked Stiletto.

"Yeah. Why? Do you know him?"

"Did they call him Redz?"

"Yeah, Redz, that's what they called him on the unit. He was locked up for robbing a bank or something."

"Oh my God! Redz . . . What happened to him?"

"Well, I found him hanging from the bunk bed with a sheet wrapped around his neck. It was like as soon as I shined my flashlight in his cell there he was . . . just hanging . . ." He nodded with sympathy. "Sorry for your loss, sista. I don't understand when somebody takes their own life. It made the news too."

Stilleto placed her hand over her mouth and began to snivel. She kept thinking that Redz was not a coward and couldn't imagine him taking his own life. Maybe it was a setup and somebody else was responsible. Then Redz' words came back to her memory and slapped her hard: *If you're not gonna do this time with me, baby, then I don't have another reason to keep breathing up in this motherfucker. Being here is like being dead. You my world, Stiletto. Without you I'm done, ma-ma.*

Teesha had their food packed to go and stayed with Stiletto all night as she mourned the love of her life, Redz, and blamed herself as if she had wrapped the sheet around Redz' neck herself.

Chapter Eighteen
THE WORST OF BOTH WORLDS

"Get the hell out of the street, asshole! You're making me late for my hair appointment." Stiletto cruised up the block in her Lexus, beeping the horn at a drunken man jaywalking.

Even though things were stressful for her ever since Redz had hung himself, Stiletto had moved on with her life. She still lived with the taste of disloyalty and did not trust any man. "Damn, it's eleven o'clock already? Damn, I am going to be late." The red light seemed as if it took decades to turn green. A cream GT Bentley pulled up on the side of her Lexus.

Stiletto noticed some guy trying to get her attention, so she rolled her window down. "What did you say? Are you talking to me?"

Spaz stuck his head out of the window. "What up, beautiful?" He smiled. "Yeah, I am talking to you. You are the only beauty in my sight."

Stiletto noticed Spaz's handsome features and remembered him from the day he approached her. She began to blush. *Damn, it's him . . . I can't believe it!*

"Yo, what's up? Why don't you pull over so I can talk to you?" Spaz's demanding words did not phase Stiletto.

"Don't I know you from somewhere?" she asked, trying to play him off.

Spaz quickly responded, "Yeah, I tried to holler at you some time ago, and you fronted on me."

"Oh yeah, I remember. I had a man at the time."

"So does that mean you're available now?"

"Maybe. I do not have time to discuss that right now. I have a hair appointment, and I am already late."

"Damn, ma. Can I at least get your phone number?"

Stiletto couldn't help smiling.

"You know, it's probably meant for us to be together because God keeps bringing you into my life."

"That was cute. Do you tell all the girls that?" asked Stiletto.

Spaz's diamonds sparkled from his chain. "I just keep it real. So what's up? Let me put your number in my phone." Spaz' phone vibrated with three missed calls from Grams.

"No, I don't think so, but you can give me your number, and I will give you a call."

Their conversation was interrupted by loud car horns from angry drivers. "Come on, man. Green light, moron!" a frustrated driver shouted.

Stiletto looked up and noticed they were holding up traffic.

Spaz yelled back, "Hold your motherfuckin' horses! Can't you see I am trying to holla at this beautiful young lady? Damn, ma, you got us holding up traffic and all that. Take my number."

Stiletto opened up her cell phone as Spaz gave her his number. She dialed the number in her phone and saved it.

"Make sure you use that number, baby girl, and don't forget about me."

Stiletto noticed the smile on Spaz's face, which reminded her of Redz. "I am going to give you a call, boo, but I got to go." Stiletto pressed her foot on the gas pedal and ran through the yellow light trying to get to her appointment. She wasn't sure if she'd call his number. Oftentimes, a new man meant a new headache.

Again, Spaz cell phone vibrated. This time it was a text message from Grams. All it said was: *Come thru asap.*

Aw shit! Here we go, Spaz thought.

Filled with several questions of what could possibly be so urgent that Grams kept blowing up his phone, Spaz made a right on the avenue and cruised through the North Philly blocks. He pulled up at the stash house, exited the car, and headed up the steps. He pulled his key out and opened the door. As he walked inside and closed the door, four nude females wearing black bandanas around their faces and latex gloves sat at a huge marble dinner table packaging keys of cocaine. .

"Yo, where the fuck is Grams and them?"

Tasha, one of the packagers, looked at Spaz with fear and lust in her eyes. "They are downstairs in the basement."

Spaz headed toward the basement. He walked toward the kitchen where the basement door was located. Two more females stood in the kitchen naked and one held a coffee pot that had steam rising from the top. Spaz walked past Natasha and smacked her on her ass. "That's right, ma. Get this motherfucking money!" Spaz walked through the door that led to the basement. Loud music echoed off the walls. Meek Mills blasted from the speakers.

"Yo, what the fuck is up with y'all?"

Slugger, Grams, and a hustler named Mell that Slugger recruited to help sell drugs were sitting on the leather sofas smoking weed and counting money.

"Yo, Spaz, come here. I want to holla at you." Grams stood up, waiting for Spaz to come closer. He gave him a hard handshake and a half a hug as they stepped to the side for privacy.

"Yo, man, what the fuck is up? What you call me down here for?"

"Yo, I need to holla at you about Slugger. He is slipping." Grams paused getting his thoughts together.

Spaz frowned and rubbed on his chin. "Tell me what happened."

"Now dig this. Your man Slugger on some other shit. First of all, he got Mell packaging up the work. Normally, you know the bitches package the work. Why is Mell down here packaging up the work? Then on top of that, the work is coming up short. Five ounces have been coming up short for the last two weeks straight. Now everybody knows Slugger is banging Mell's sister. Now I put some cameras in here and I looked at the tapes and I got your boy Mell stealing work. And your man Slugger letting it ride. So what I am telling you is Slugger is getting soft. I don't trust him anymore. I will rock that nigga if I have to."

Spaz grimaced because one thing he hated was a thief. "Hold up, Grams. Are you sure about this?"

"Sure? I am positive. We can go upstairs right now and look at the tape."

Spaz's lips tightened. "Come on. Let's go check this shit out."

The two men walked up the basement steps to the third floor. Slugger and Mell remained downstairs on the couch playing NBA Live. Spaz and Grams took a seat on the black leather sofa and watched the footage on the 50-inch plasma. Spaz lit up a Dutch, inhaled the marijuana smoke, and blew it out of his nose. On the TV screen, Mell reached on a table full of drugs and placed the missing ounces of drugs into his pockets. The tape played several times on different days, and each time the same amounts of drugs were taken.

Spaz's eyebrows rose to the top of his head. "I can't believe this snake motherfucker!" He rose to his feet and stormed out the door.

Grams followed Spaz back to the basement.

Heated by the video footage, Spaz walked up to Slugger and Mell. "Yo, I hate to interrupt this game, but I need to holla at both of y'all." Spaz unzipped his leather jacket and placed it on the pool table. "Yo, Mell, come here. Let me holla at you for a minute."

Mell rose to his feet and walked up to Spaz. "What's up, G?"

"Ain't nothing, player. What's up with you, man?" Spaz reached on his hip and pulled out a chrome .45. "Yo, Mell, you like this new gat I just bought?"

Mell nervously replied, "Yeah, man, that jawn is hot."

Spaz smiled. "It's hot, right?" Spaz quickly smacked Mell on the forehead with the gun, knocking him to the floor.

Mell rolled around holding his head with blood dripping down his fingers. "Yo, man, why the fuck did you do that? What did I do?"

"Pussy, you know why I did that, you fucking thief!"

Slugger shook his head as Spaz began kicking Mell.

"Nigga, get the fuck up!"

Mell stumbled to his feet.

"Take your clothes off, pussy!"

Mell began taking off his clothes.

Spaz reached in his pocket and took his money. "This is my money you have been stealing!" He noticed a bag of PCP fall from Mell's pocket. "Oh, this is why you have been stealing from me? You're buying wet? You were smoking angel dust?" Spaz smacked Mell again in his head with the .45.

Mell fell hard to the ground with blood dripping from his face.

"Ay yo, Slugger, get the fuck over here!"

Slugger walked slowly to Spaz.

"Yo, this is your responsibility. You were fucking his sister, right?"

Slugger looked nervous. "Damn, what are you talking about?"

"Yo, Grams, go get the carpet from the back."

Grams walked to the back and grabbed a huge roll of carpet and put it on the floor where Mell lay.

"Yeah, this disloyal piece of shit has been stealing from me, and he's your responsibility, so you are going to kill him."

Slugger hesitantly grabbed the gat from Spaz while Mell started crying for his life.

"Come on, man. Please, man, don't do it. Why are you trippin'? Come on, man. Please, please, please."

"Yo, Slugger, shoot him now!"

Grams gripped Mell by his neck and punched him in the mouth. "I ain't neva liked you any way."

Slugger put the gat to Mell's head and hesitated.

"Come on, man. Why are you doing this to me, man? Please don't kill me, man. I'll get the money back."

Spaz grew furious. "Money? You think this is about money? This is about respect, and you don't have respect for my business. You chose death over honor. I don't play those games here, and you are going to see what happens to disrespectful motherfuckers like you. It's a rap! Yo, Slugger, pop him!"

Slugger let off a shot into Mell's chest.

He began screaming and hollering. "Aahhh! Aaaaah, you shot me!"

"Finish off this clown so we can get the fuck out of here!"

Slugger pumped more shots into Mell's body, putting an end to his life.

Spaz looked into Slugger's eyes. "Empty the whole clip on him!"

Slugger let off loud rounds of ammunition into Mell's lifeless body.

"Now, you motherfuckers clean this mess up! And from now on, Grams, you run this shit because Slugger is too pussy whipped to run the business. Step your game up. You fallin' off."

Blood covered the carpet on the basement floor as Grams and Slugger wrapped Mell's body up.

"Make sure you roll this motherfucker up and get his ass out of here." Spaz walked to the pool table and grabbed his jacket. "Damn, he got blood all over my brand new butter leather."

Spaz approached Slugger. "This can never happen again."

Chapter Nineteen
CONTAGIOUS ENERGY

Stiletto felt a bit disappointed after she called Spaz's cell phone and he did not pick up, so she decided to call her cousin. "Hello. What's up, Teesha? Girl, you will not believe who I bumped into today?"

"Who, girl? Tell me."

"Spaz. Remember the dude that tried to holla sometime back when he was with your boy Slugger?"

"Oh yeah, that's right. I remember. I am glad for you. It's time for you to give those cookies up. You know Spaz is getting plenty of paper."

"He gave me his number today while I was on my way to the hair salon. He was looking good in that new GT coupe. I just called him, and he did not pick up the phone."

"Girl, you better call him again before another bitch beats you to the punch. He is a winner."

"I am not trying to get caught up in love again." Her phone beeped.

"I know what you mean, girl."

"I will call you later. This is him calling me on the other line." Stiletto ended her call with Teesha and answered her other line. "Hello."

"Yo, did somebody just call Spaz?"

"Yes, it's Stiletto."

"Stiletto, where do I know you from?"

"I met you today at the red light."

"Oh shit, my bad. What's up, baby?"

"Not much, just laying back in the tub, chilling."

"Oh yeah. Do you need some company over there?"

"I might, but not tonight."

"All right, well listen . . . I would like to spend some time with you tomorrow if you're available. I was thinking of hanging out at a nice sports bar or lounge so we can get to know each other."

"That sounds good."

"All right. So what time will you be available?"

"How does 8:00 p.m. sound?"

"That sounds good, baby girl. I got some business to take care of right now. I will see you tomorrow at eight."

Stiletto hung up the phone with a smile and began to fantasize about their first intimate encounter. She relaxed in the hot bubble bath while listening to Alicia Key's single "No One." *Damn, I forgot to ask him if he had a girl! Redz and his baby and his death was more than enough drama for one relationship.* I'd have to kill a nigga for real.

Around 7:55 p.m., a horn beeped, which startled Stiletto. She was surprised that Spaz was actually on time.

Stiletto headed out the door and walked to the cream Bentley GT. She smiled as Spaz kissed her on the cheek.

"Hello, beautiful. You look amazing!" he said with his eyes glued on her physique.

"Thank you. You look great yourself."

Spaz took Stiletto's hand. He opened the passenger door and waited for her to sit comfortably before he shut the door. Stiletto took note of his suave style. He wore a tan Gucci blazer with dark blue True Religion jeans and tan Gucci sneakers. She was fascinated with how good he looked. It was almost like the waves in his hair matched his swagger.

"So what line of business you in? Selling drugs, robbing, and extortion?" she asked curiously.

"No, I'm not a drug dealer. I'm a businessman," said Spaz, then he climbed in the driver's seat.

"Mm hmm." She smirked. *This guy must think I'm stupid. Lord, why am I so attracted to ballers and gangsters?*

Thirty minutes later, Spaz and Stiletto arrived at their destination. The valet attendant knew Spaz and called him by name as he and Stiletto exited the car and headed into Tops-Up Lounge. The two walked into the spot where the majority of the crowd was Italian. They all hugged Spaz and shook his hand. He was the man and Stiletto could tell. She felt honored to be in his presence. The two were seated at a small table in the back of the restaurant, and the waitress immediately brought over a chilled bottle of Moet. Spaz and Stiletto toasted to new beginnings and a life of happiness and continued success. Many people kept walking up to the table and greeting Spaz. Within five minutes, their waiter returned and told Spaz that Sticky Scilionni was ready to meet with him.

"Excuse me for a minute. I am going to talk to a good friend of mine. Okay, baby?"

"I'll be here when you get back," she said, exposing her pretty smile.

Sticky Scilionni was sitting in his office smoking on a cigar when Spaz walked in. "Sticky, what's going on, man?"

"I'm fine, kid. Have a seat. You want a cigar?"

"Sure, boss."

"Let me give you a light, kid."

Spaz held the cigar in his mouth as he leaned closer to the fire. The end of the cigar turned red as smoke rose. Spaz inhaled the smoke and leaned back in his chair. "So what's up, Sticky? You seem to be in a good mood. What's going on?" Spaz blew the smoke out of his mouth slowly. "I can tell when you got something going on. Tell me what's up?"

Sticky smiled in appreciation. "You know me too well, kid. Listen, let's get down to business. Right now I'm stuck with a lot of work."

Spaz's eyes grew larger. "So what are you saying?"

"I am saying, kid, I need you to open up more shops. I got a thousand keys that I need you to take care of for me."

Spaz's heart dropped. "I think I can manage that, but I want them for a cheaper price."

"Cheaper price! Come on, kid. Stop busting my balls."

"Sticky, I am already moving one hundred keys a week at 15k each. Now you're trying to drop a thousand on me. You know the economics of this game. The more you purchase, the cost decreases, so what do you mean 'busting your balls'?" Spaz inhaled more of the Cuban cigar smoke.

Sticky laughed. "This kid is unbelievable," he said to one of his gunmen. "I think I taught you too much. All right, kid, you win. As usual, you negotiate the best deal for yourself. I'll have them deliver the work to you tomorrow morning at 11:00 a.m." Sticky reached on the table and grabbed the camera monitor remote and watched the view of Stiletto's beautiful face. "And who is this gorgeous companion you have with you tonight?"

Spaz faced the monitor and grinned. "That's my new boo. I think she has the potential to stick around for a while."

Sticky licked his lips. "Not bad, kid. Take care of the beautiful lady. That's the key. Treat her like a queen, and she will never leave your side. But don't treat her too well, and she'll shit all over you. That's all I have for tonight. Enjoy your evening, and I will talk to you later."

Spaz stood up and shook Sticky's hand and put out the cigar in the ashtray. He walked back to the table to sit with Stiletto.

"I hope I didn't keep you waiting too long."

Stiletto smiled. "Not too long, but I was beginning to miss you."

A beautiful Italian waitress greeted him as soon as he sat down. "Good evening, Spaz. What will you have tonight?"

"I will have the shrimp pasta dinner." He turned to Stiletto. "Baby, what would you like?"

Stiletto ordered the steak and potatoes. As they waited for dinner, they began to talk about life. Stiletto took a deep breath and looked in Spaz's eyes. "Do you have a girlfriend?"

"What would you consider a girlfriend? I have a lot of friends who are girls."

"Okay. Well, do you have a special lady that you spend a lot of time with, and if anything happened to you, would she feel pain?"

Spaz smiled. "My mother but she passed away."

"I'm so sorry to hear that," she said, reaching for his hand.

"No, it's okay. Please continue," said Spaz.

Stiletto knew she was facing a challenge, based on his sarcastic answers. "Let me take this a bit further . . . a lady that you are sexually involved with and are possibly considering as your wife."

Silence grew at their table.

"When I look at you, that's what comes to my mind, a beautiful woman that I would consider as my wife."

She remained expressionless. "As I look in your eyes, my heart tells me that you are sincere, but my past relationships make me unsure. From what I have seen tonight, I feel convinced that you're a straight-up guy and that makes me want to be with you right here right now. But before we go any further, I want to be sure that if I give you my heart, you must promise not to hurt me."

Spaz smiled. "Baby, if you give me your heart, I promise you I wouldn't drop it."

They shared a very sensual kiss that lasted about thirty seconds. Spaz and Stiletto were kissing when the waitress approached the table with their dinner. The kiss was so intense that the two did not notice her arrival.

The waitress made a few sounds to get their attention. "Hum um."

Spaz looked up at the waitress. "Sweetheart, can you prepare our dinners for takeout?"

"Sure, no problem. Do you need anything else?"

"One more thing, please have my car brought up because everything else I need is right here."

Stiletto smiled and took another sip of her champagne.

Four minutes later, the waitress came back to the table with the meals packed and handed them to Spaz. The two left the table in bliss. Spaz shook a few hands on his way out of the restaurant and headed for the door.

Sticky and Nikki walked toward the exit and watched as the valet attendant stepped out of Spaz's Bentley GT. Spaz waited patiently.

"Un-fucking believable," Sticky mumbled. "Hey, hey, Spaz, come here."

Spaz escorted Stiletto into the front seat, and then headed over to where Sticky and Nikki stood.

"What's the matter with you?" Sticky asked.

"What are you talking about?" Spaz said.

"What are you, stupid? What's the matter with you, kid?"

"What did I do wrong?"

"How many times have I told you, stay low-key? Get rid of this fucking car. It's an indictment on wheels. I don't want to see it here. Get rid of it."

"But I just bought it."

"I don't care. Get rid of it!"

"Okay. Okay," Spaz said, heading back to his new car.

Sticky whispered to Nikki Montagna, "Keep a close eye on those two."

Nikki Montagna shook his head in agreement. "No problem, Sticky."

Agent Mark Rizzo watched from a parked car in disbelief. "Who the hell is this black kid talking to Sticky? I mean this fucking guy eats dinner in Sticky's restaurant, gets love from everybody in the place, and then jumps in a Bentley GT? He must be a famous rap artist."

Chapter Twenty
SEXUAL FIREWORKS

The Bentley GT drove off into the night with the couple laughing and joking as Power 99 FM played Force MD's "Tender Love." Spaz pulled up to Stiletto's house and parked. He began to separate the food and passed Stiletto her meal.

Stiletto smiled and spoke in a soft tone. "Aren't you going to walk me to the door? It's pretty late."

Spaz smiled. "Sure, baby. Sit tight and I will be right over to open your door." Spaz stepped out of the car and went to the passenger side. He opened the door, then grabbed the food from her hand as she got out of the car. The two walked slowly holding hands until they arrived at her front door. When they got to the door, Stiletto reached in her purse to grab her keys.

Spaz leaned toward Stiletto for a deep passionate kiss. "Goodnight, beautiful."

"Goodnight, boo." She blushed.

"I had a good time. Hopefully we can do this every weekend," said Spaz.

"That would be nice." She smiled. *He is so damn fine.*

"Okay, perfect," he said, walking away.

"Spaz, wait!" she yelled.

Spaz walked toward Stiletto. "What's up?"

"Can you come in and check around to make sure everything is okay inside before you leave?"

Spaz stared at her juicy lips and kissed them once more. "Of course, baby. You know I got your back." Spaz opened the door and walked in first. "Wait, stay back. I think I hear something."

"Are you serious?" Stiletto looked startled.

He suddenly turned around. "Booo!"

Stiletto's heart dropped and she cringed with fear.

Spaz began laughing out loud. "I was just playing."

Stiletto slammed the door closed to break the tension. "Would you like something to drink?" she asked.

"Sure," he said, walking so close to Stiletto that he could smell the peppermint on her breath. Spaz kissed Stiletto's soft lips and she returned the favor. Each second grew more intense as they began snatching each other's clothes off. Spaz picked her up and carried her to the bedroom and placed her naked body on the soft bed.

He was amazed at the combination of attractive qualities: her thick hourglass figure, her smooth caramel complexion, and Chinese hairstyle. Even her toes turned him on. He noticed her birthmark below her belly button that was shaped like an arrow that pointed toward her wet vagina.

"Do you see something you like?" she asked, inspiring more lust from the sweet sound of her voice. Stiletto slowly set apart her thighs.

"Wow, that's beautiful," he complimented her pearl tongue and went head first for a closer look. "Damn." He smiled, placing his lips and tongue inside of her wet tunnel of love.

"Tell me how it tastes?" she said while grabbing the back of his head with both of her hands, stroking his wavy hair pattern.

"It tastes like strawberries," he responded, squeezing her soft ass cheeks. The tip of his tongue tap danced around the edges of her clit.

Stiletto enjoyed her tongue massage and was on the verge of going into a creamy explosion, but Spaz suddenly stopped and lay on his back. "Why you stop?" she asked with her legs shaking.

"Shut up and get over here," he demanded.

Stiletto climbed her flawless body on top of Spaz and took notice of the huge tattoo across his chest. She began to trace each letter with her tongue. "I knew you were with the BBF. Why you lie?"

"I just didn't want to scare you away," said Spaz and relaxed his hands behind his head.

"Boy please! You not the first gangster I been with and you won't be the last," she said, wetting his nipples with her tongue. "I want you to put my name over here," she teased.

"Oh yeah? Turn around and let me French kiss that pussy."

Stiletto reversed her body into a 69 position. She felt her pooh nanny getting wet each minute.

"Aahh," she moaned with her eyes closed, feeling the pleasurable sensation with each stroke of his tongue.

Spaz's hands crawled up Stiletto's back and pressed down on her shoulders. She was focused on climaxing, not noticing Spaz's swollen love stick needing her attention. Immediately, she began sucking on his dick slowly, and enjoying every slurp while getting pleased at the same time.

Stiletto felt herself about to cum once more. "Ah!" She locked her thighs on Spaz's face and sat straight up on her knees. "Ah!" She shivered, and suddenly Spaz stopped again.

"Why you keep stopping?" she asked, dissatisfied. She wanted to go to heaven but kept being greeted by the Grim reaper.

"Shut up and lay down," he said romantically, then pushed her on her back.

Stiletto squealed as he climbed between her legs.

"Fuck me."

"That's what you want?"

"Yes."

"Say please."

"Please fuck me!"

Spaz pushed his throbbing penis inside of her.

"Uh! Don't hurt me," she begged as Spaz slammed twelve inches of passion in and out of her. "Oh, right there! Don't stop!"

Spaz explored her mansion of love, entering sacred rooms, touching all four walls. Stiletto's moans and screams made Spaz go deeper. "Damn, this pussy good."

"You like it, daddy?" she asked with a pretty sex face. Her firm breasts bounced up and down with each stroke from Spaz's love machine. The sex was wet and pleasurable.

"Damn, I'm 'bout to cum," Spaz said with a forehead full of sweat.

"Me too, ahh!" Stiletto screamed. The two lovers exploded, releasing sexual fireworks.

Ten minutes later, Stiletto bit her tongue and began to moan as Spaz began rubbing her clit with his thumb. He grew hard and pushed his dick back inside her. He took slow strokes for the next twenty minutes. Sounds of sex echoed throughout the house and they both began enjoying their second orgasm. Sweat poured from their naked bodies as they relaxed, catching their breath.

Stiletto enjoyed her night of passion as they both pumped themselves into multiple orgasms. Spaz grabbed her body and turned her to the doggy style position and stroked in and out as hard as he could.

"Enjoy it, baby. It's all yours!" Spaz smacked her hard on her luscious ass and began to climax once more.

"That was amazing," said Stiletto.

Spaz sat up on the edge of the bed and reached into his pocket, pulled out a bag of weed, and rolled it up. He took the lighter and lit the tip and inhaled the smoke into his nose. Stiletto was proud to have a man like Spaz as her eyes followed him around the room.

"Yo, you want to hit this?"

"No, I'm cool. I don't smoke."

"Oh yeah? Peer pressure is a motherfucker." Spaz blew smoke in her face and chuckled.

Stiletto fanned the smoke with her hand. "Stop playing, boy. I don't get down like that."

The sound of Spaz's cell phone interrupted their playful conversation.

"Man, let me see who the hell this is." Spaz picked up the cell phone. "Hello?"

Grams was on the other end. "Yo, what's up?"

"Ain't nothing. We need some more cars on the lot," Gams said, using the code word for purchasing more drugs.

"Can you hold off until the morning?"

"Morning? You know we grynd until the world end, nigga. You losing ya' hunger, bro."

Spaz stared at Stiletto and shook his head. "Shit!" He didn't want to lose focus. "All right I'll be there in forty-five minutes." Spaz hung up the phone and began getting dressed.

Stiletto frowned. "Where are you going?"

"I'm sorry to be leaving so soon, but I forgot about this meeting."

"A meeting? I thought we were going to spend the night together."

"I did too. This totally slipped my mind. It was unexpected, and I hope you understand."

"Well, do you want me to go with you?"

"No, baby, I can take care of this. You just take care of that beautiful body, and I will catch up with you tomorrow."

Stiletto felt hurt and rejected. *He's not feeling me!* Stiletto rose to her feet. "I *knew* you were just like the rest of these no-good ass niggas! You come here, romance me, and take off! That shit is not cool. You will not get another chance to play me like this. As a matter of fact, you are not leaving." Stiletto grabbed Spaz's keys from him. "You told me earlier you wouldn't hurt me. I guess that was game."

He snatched his keys back from her hand swiftly and pulled Stiletto in his arms. "Let's get one thing clear: I am not trying to hurt you. It's just when it comes down to business, I have to handle it. I can't let anything come before that. I am feeling you, and I hope this will not be a problem. I can honestly say that this will not be a one-night stand. I feel that we have connected. I know this can become greater, you dig me?"

Stiletto took a deep breath as she began to feel guilty about overreacting. "I'm sorry, boo. It's just that I have been hurt before, and I am not trying to cross that road again."

Spaz looked deep into her eyes. "You have to trust me, baby. You have to believe me and everything else will fall into place." Spaz pushed his face against her warm lips.

"I have to go. I'll call you later." Spaz headed for the door. *Damn, shorty going to be a problem.* Spaz turned to see Stiletto coming toward him with a gun in her hand. His heart dropped and his eyes grew wide. *Is she about to shoot me?*

Stiletto turned the gun backward. "You left this under the pillow."

This bitch is crazy!

Twenty-one
SEEDS FROM ROTTEN FRUIT

Martini was in a deep sleep wearing a short Victoria's Secret satin nightgown. Her huge bedroom was decorated with paintings and furniture from the Z Gallery with a Sony 50-inch HD television. Her son began to cry from his baby crib. Martini woke up from her deep sleep and walked toward her son. "Is my baby hungry? Let me get you a bottle." She walked to the kitchen and prepared a warm bottle of milk for her son, Yasmeen. While preparing the milk, Yasmeen cried louder and louder. "I will be right there, baby. Just give me a few seconds." Martini squirted the milk on her palm to test the temperature. Suddenly the cry was replaced with laughter. Martini walked back into the bedroom and dropped the baby bottle. "What the fuck! You scared the shit out of me!" She was frightened.

"I am tired of you coming in here all times of the night, scaring us." Her foot always tapped the floor simultaneously when she was angry.

"I was out making moves and all that. You know I got to go hard out here in the streets in order to provide this expensive ass roof over your head."

She rolled her eyes. "And stop popping up from nowhere scaring us," she added, picking up the bottle from the floor. Martini went into the bathroom to rinse it off.

"You're the only one scared. My son is happy to see me. My little man must have been expecting me," said Spaz.

Martini entered the bedroom complaining. "So where were you, over one of your bitches' house?"

"Come on, Martini. Don't start this bullshit."

"What do you mean 'don't start this bullshit?' I am tired of you putting me through all this drama."

Spaz sat down on the bed with his son. "Give me the bottle so I can feed him."

Martini passed the bottle to Spaz in anger. The baby drank the milk with urgency. "Now how many times are you going to promise me that you are going to leave this drug game alone? We have enough. Have you ever thought about what will happen to us if you get locked up? I mean, damn, you want me and your son to come see you locked up? I'll tell you right now, I am not coming to see you in jail."

Spaz frowned up. "Yo, why do you keep talking about jail? I'm not going to jail! I got the best attorneys in the city. I am not planning to stay in this game forever. By the end of the year we will be moving to sunny California." Spaz rose to his feet and headed to the shower. "So stop trippin'."

"Sunny California. Hunh! I won't be holding my breath. That's for damn sure," Martini said, snatching the now empty bottle from Spaz. "I know you better than you know yourself."

"You keep thinking that, ma." Spaz kissed her on her right shoulder and then walked into the bathroom and closed the door.

The next morning Spaz awoke to the smell of pancakes, turkey bacon, and cheese eggs. "Damn, that shit smells delicious. I can already taste those buttermilk pancakes!" Spaz walked to the kitchen table wearing his silk Versace robe and matching slippers.

"Good morning, boo. I made you breakfast."

"I can smell it, baby. It smells delicious. I thought I was dreaming."

Martini smiled as Spaz kissed her on the cheek. "Enjoy your meal, boo."

Spaz started to eat his breakfast as he turned on the *CNN* news.

"Hello, this is Monica Larson reporting live from City Hall in downtown Philadelphia where the crime rate has risen. Philadelphia is now the murder capital of the United States. Statistics indicate that there are more people being violently murdered on the streets of the City of Brotherly Love than in the war in Afghanistan."

Spaz's eyes were glued to the television. He finished his breakfast with a cold glass of orange juice. Within minutes his phone began ringing.

"Hello." Spaz heard a familiar voice on the other end of the phone. "Yo, who is this?"

"Oh, you don't remember my voice now, huh? You took me out to dinner last night."

Martini picked up the empty plate and gave Spaz a side glance. "What's up, Grams? Are you all right?"

Stiletto was confused. "Why are you talking to me as if I am one of your homies? You must be around one of your bitches?"

"Yes, you're right. I'll be there in forty-five minutes. I'll see you then," he said ignoring Stiletto's statement.

Spaz hung up the phone, walked into the bathroom, showered and got dressed.

Martini stared at Spaz as he sprayed on his cologne and grabbed his keys. "Where the fuck are you going?"

Spaz kissed Martini on the cheek. "I have to go, baby. I have some business to take care of this morning. I will be back later."

"Mmm hmm, baby. See you later," Martini said, unhappy about him leaving. She immediately got on the phone and made a call. "Hey, girl. I just called to see what's up with you today. I miss you," she said, glancing at Spaz' back as he closed the door behind him. She opened the door and peeped out to make sure Spaz was far from listening distance.

"Yeah, he's gone now. So when am I going to see you? I miss you so much, daddy." Martini grinned.

Gunmen from the Black Boss Family stood on Twentieth and Brown watching the area for jackers as Grams and Slugger unloaded gym bags filled with kilos of cocaine. Each bag was taken to different locations. Nineteenth Street made about $100,000 a day. Twenty-Fifth Street made $50,000 a day. Spaz had hustlers coming from all over the city to buy his product. Before he knew it, the thousand keys that Sticky gave him were gone, and Spaz had all the money that he owed. Grams was the collector and when hustlers didn't pay, Grams blew their brains out. They were left as examples and not too many people had problems paying after that. They got the message. Spaz wasn't taking any shorts.

Spaz cruised up the avenue in his Maserati and called Stiletto's telephone number. "What's up, ma?"

"Don't 'what's *up,* ma' me! Now you're calling me back after I have been calling your phone for hours. You must have just left one of your bitches."

Spaz shook his head. "Why are you tripping? I'm on my way over there to holler at you."

"Oh, no you're not. You're not going to be laying up with them whores then come and have sex with me. There are diseases out here, you know?"

"Stiletto, come on."

"Yeah, whateva. You niggas make me sick."

"If anything, I make you feel a lot better than sick. That's the truth. What you want me to do? Do you want me to beg?"

There was something about Spaz that she was attracted to in a major way. She never fell this quickly for any man, so she decided to meet with Spaz to express her feelings. She hoped he would feel the same way. "Well, you have to at least give me an hour to get dressed."

"Okay, cool. I'll pick you up in about an hour. I got some moves to make anyway." The two hung up the phone.

Sixty minutes later, Spaz and Stiletto rode up the avenue.

"Anyway, nigga, you think you slick calling me Grams on the phone. What you was around your bitch and you tried to play it off like you was talking to one of your boys?" yelled Stiletto.

"What? You trippin'. I don't know what you talking about," Spaz responded.

"Nigga, you ain't got to lie. You called me Grams. My name is Stiletto, boo," she said with a smirk.

"Hold up. Chill."

"No, nigga, chill don't pay bills."

"Wait, look, I think somebody following us." He glanced through the rearview mirror and noticed an all-black Lincoln Town Car trailing them.

"Oh, hell naw! Who the fuck is that, Spaz?"

"I don't know." He turned up Ridge Avenue, and the Lincoln continued to follow him. Spaz reached into his pocket and pulled out his cell phone and dialed Grams' number. "Grams, where y'all at?"

"We're on Twentieth Street. Why? What's up with you?"

"I'm calling because someone is following me."

"Who following you?"

"I don't know."

"Well, what's up? What do you want me to do?"

"Listen, meet me on Girard and Ridge Avenue. When you see me coming through, just get in position to blast these stupid motherfuckers out of their misery!"

"I got you, my nigga. Don't even sweat it. It's a wrap."

Spaz hung up the phone. The Lincoln continued to follow.

Stiletto grew nervous from listening to the conversation. "Somebody is following us, Spaz?"

"Just lean your seat back and relax."

"My life is in danger. How can I relax?"

"Stiletto, listen to me. Reach in that glove compartment and give me my gun."

Stiletto opened the glove compartment.

"Push that green button on the side."

She pushed the button and a stash spot opened up with two pistols lying there. Stiletto grabbed the Desert Eagle and gave it to Spaz, then she grabbed the .45.

"Yo, what you doing?"

"My life is in danger. I'm protecting myself."

Spaz became alarmed. "Stop playing with that shit. You don't know how to handle a gun."

The left side of her face rose with an expression of disagreement as she cocked the .45 back. "You don't know me very well."

Spaz smiled and drove slowly up the block. The Lincoln turned the corner trailing Spaz. He pumped his brakes, and the tinted Lincoln crashed into the back of his Maserati. Then he sped up the block as Grams and Slugger and the twins came out of the alleyway shooting at the Lincoln. The driver of the Lincoln lost control of the steering wheel as bullets showered the vehicle. Huge holes and broken glass decorated the car.

Spaz put the car in park and yelled at Stiletto, "Wait in the car!"

"Okay, but be careful," she said nervously.

Spaz crept toward the Lincoln. The horn continuously blew from the driver's head being stuck to the steering wheel. A huge bullet hole filled the back of his head.

The passenger jumped out squeezing a MAC-11 with blood dripping from his mouth. "Motherfuckers!"

Grams and Slugger took cover behind parked cars. Bullets flew violently in their direction, breaking car windows and tearing through parked cars. An innocent bystander caught a slug in the neck, causing blood to sprinkle in the air as he fell to his death. Spaz moved from car to car, creeping on his target, which was in clear view. Without being noticed, Spaz took a good aim at his chest and squeezed the trigger. The shots caught the gunman in his chest and shoulder, knocking him to the ground. Spaz moved in closer. *Who the fuck is this?* He stood over him with gun in hand, executioner style. He took a deep breath, watching his prey gasp for air. Blood pooled underneath him. His trigger budged.

"Spaz, are you okay?" The sound of Stiletto's voice took his attention off his target.

"Yo, didn't I tell you to stay in the fucking car!" Spaz turned toward Stiletto.

"I thought you got shot or something." Stiletto noticed the injured gunman regaining consciousness, clutching his MAC-11 and slowly aiming back.

"Watch out, Spaz!" Stiletto pushed him aside and fired seven shots into the gunman's stomach. His body shook back and forth. Three more shots caught him in the forehead. Blood squirted on the concrete.

Stiletto's body quaked as she stood in place with her gun still aimed at her target.

"Who the fuck are these guys?" Spaz said aloud as he gazed into the dead man's brown eyes.

"An even better question is who sent them?" Stiletto asked as her bottom lip trembled.

"You're right." Because the men were Italian, Spaz thought of Sticky right away. *Nah, couldn't be*, he thought. *Could he?*

Chapter Twenty-two
ONE SLIP AWAY FROM HELL

Spaz took a seat behind his desk and Stiletto sat on his lap still in shock and wondering if the murder she'd just committed was something that she was willing to do on a regular just to be with Spaz.

"Everything gone be a'ight," Spaz said, massaging her back.

Slugger and Grams took their seats on the sofa.

Spaz broke the silence. "Grams, pass me a light."

Grams reached in his pocket and threw Spaz a bic.

"Yo, I need soldiers on the street finding out who the fuck was responsible for me getting shot at."

"It's a done deal," said Slugger.

Grams noticed Stiletto looking worried. "What's up, mommy? You okay?"

Spaz intervened. "She good. She just a little shook up."

The murder replayed in Stiletto's head. "Where's the bathroom?" she asked quickly.

"It's over there." Spaz pointed.

Stiletto ran to the restroom, kneeled over the toilet, and vomited.

"Yo, you think she gone crack under pressure?" Slugger asked Spaz.

"I hope not. I would hate to have to kill her," Grams said.

"Ain't nobody killing nobody. She good, trust me. She got a lot of heart."

"Okay, but you already know how I get down."

The conversation was interrupted by Spaz's cell phone.

"Hello?"

"Hey, kid. How are you?"

"I'm good. What's up with you, Sticky? I didn't recognize this number."

"Well, we got a problem. I need you to come to my office ASAP."

"I will be right over." Spaz hung up the phone and took a deep breath. "Yo, that was Sticky. I got to go holla at him."

Grams said, "I don't trust that motherfucka."

"Calm down, killa," said Spaz.

Stiletto came out the bathroom with all eyes on her. "I'll be okay. I just needed a minute.

Mark Rizzo's eyes widened when Spaz pulled up to Tops-Up Lounge, and he climbed out of a Lincoln Navigator and headed inside. Cameras began flashing as he walked inside the spot.

Sticky sat in his office smoking a Cuban cigar when Spaz entered. Several of Sticky's men stood in the room holding guns.

"Have a seat," he demanded.

"So how is everything, Sticky?"

"Good, kid, not bad. My lawyer's going to beat this case they got pending on me. But we have a little problem."

"And what might that be?"

Sticky began to laugh. "You hear this kid? Ha! You like surprises, right kid?"

"That depends on if it's my birthday or not."

"Well, it's not your birthday, kid. It's also not the Polo brothers' birthday either. But I do not want them to see their next ones. Those fucking cocksuckers refused to pay their taxes to me. I don't want the money anymore. I want you and your family to take care of them morons. I have to set an example with them, or others might think they can piss all over me. They will be at Nick's pool hall on Saturday. I want you to get there early, play some games of pool, and when they get there, I want you to execute those fuckers!"

Sticky rose to his feet and walked closely to Spaz and rested his palm on his shoulder. "Kid, I got love for you and a lot of guys are going to have to get whacked. I want to see you around, kid."

Spaz stared in Sticky's eyes. "I will definitely be here. I have no plans to go anywhere anytime soon." Spaz walked out the door while Sticky stared at him.

Agent Rizzo took more pictures as Spaz exited the lounge and entered his car. "I will find out exactly who you are and what you are doing hanging around Mr. Sticky Scilionni."

Chapter Twenty-three
BLOODY FOOTSTEPS

It was the Fourth of July and fireworks decorated the skies. Grams and Spaz had a meeting in a secluded area under the Delaware Bridge.

"So what's up, Grams?" Spaz asked.

"You know . . . maintaining, holding shit down," said Grams, puffing on a cigar filled with weed. "Swa! Swa!" was the sound he made while smoking a blunt. "Shit getting crazy with Cola," Grams admitted.

"What's the problem with her?"

"She's been out of pocket ever since her girl Princess got murdered. But I don't know, man. It's like since she the first lady of the BBF too, she letting the shit go to her head," said Grams.

"You trained her. I told you not to allow her on too many murders. Now you done created a monsta." Spaz knew that Cola was going to be a problem.

"If we don't do something about her, she's going to get us indicted."

"So what happened to make you come to this conclusion?"

"I take this crazy bitch out to Virginia with me to deliver a shipment. So I got her to drive while I put my seat back and chilled."

Grams and Cola were on I-95 on their way to Virginia.

"Nigga, I know you not going to sleep. You gonna stay up with me while I drive?" she asked, switching lanes.

"What the fuck I look like? Your navigation system? I'm tired as shit," Grams said, closing his eyes. "Just wake me up when we get there."

"You know what, Grams? I can't with you. I'm not even going to go there. Take your ass to sleep then."

"Damn, can a nigga get some sleep?"

"That's just why I can't stand your ass," she said, turning the volume up on the radio.

R. Kelly's "Slow Dance" calmed the mood.

Cola was trying to pick a fight with Grams. No matter how many times Cola flirted with Grams, he never had sex with her. He just ignored her and relaxed until he fell asleep.

Cola was growing impatient. She wanted to get this trip over with. So she sped up. "Damn, this muthafucka is fast." Cola got careless, going over the speed limit and switching from lane to lane.

Grams was fast asleep. He'd been awake for two days. He been popping Molly's and partying with Cola. He just wanted to rest, but the sound of cop sirens caught his attention.

"Yo, what the fuck? You speeding! Aw, ma, we got bricks in the trunk!"

"Shut your scary ass up. You think I'm a let this cop take us to jail?" she said, placing her gun on her lap.

"Yo, put that shit up!" he yelled.

"What! Just chill."

Grams contemplated what was to occur as Cola pulled the car over on the side of the highway. "You dumb muthafucka, speeding," said Grams as he waited patiently for the officer to approach them.

"Don't do anything stupid," he told her.

"Who me?" she responded with a devilish smirk.

Grams shook his head. "I'm not trying to go to jail,"
he said.

The officer approached the car cautiously, keeping his
hand on his gun handle. "License and registration,
please," said the officer. "You were going way over the
speed limit."

"Oh, I'm sorry, officer. I didn't notice."

The police officer noticed a half a blunt in the astray.
"Excuse me, ma'am. You mind stepping out the car for
me?"

"What is that on your face, officer?" Cola asked.

The officer said, "On my face? What is it?"

"A bullet, muthafucka!" One loud shot tore the
officer's head from his neck.

Cola drove away at full speed in a Dodge Charger.

Grams took another hit of the weed, bringing him back
to the present. He inhaled the weed smoke. "I'm lucky to
be standing here telling you this story, Spaz. That bitch is
out of control. I'm ready to give her, her sleeping pills,"
said Grams. "You better do something with her before I
kill that crazy bitch. She fuck around and get us all life
behind bars."

"Okay, let me talk to her. Because we don't need no
extra heat. We already hot as it is," said Spaz. The two
shook hands and went their separate ways.

Spaz couldn't get the phrase "life behind bars" out of
his mind. He needed to talk to Cola ASAP

That Thursday, Cola met Spaz at his office at the BBF
headquarters in North Philly. The office was still the same
as it was when Reel was boss. The only thing new was the

stereo. *I hate this place.* Spaz never felt comfortable in this particular office because he knew that Chips' spirit was lurking inside. His conscience was guilty about killing Chips. The knocks at the door took him out the moment.

"Come in," he said, adjusting his voice.

"What's up, Spaz?" Cola greeted Spaz with hugs and smiles, looking fabulous in a tight cat suit, exposing her video vixen body.

"It's not a thing. What's the situation?" He hugged her.

"Damn, you smelling all good," she complimented.

"Have a seat." Spaz sat next to her, lighting a cigar full of weed. "Here, hit this."

Cola inhaled the intoxicant and the two began to converse.

"Here's the problem: you're making a lot of bad decisions that is costing the family money for lawyers and possible jail time. I cannot let that happen. You understand me?" Spaz said with a serious facial expression.

"Oh, you so sexy when you mad," she flirted.

Spaz gripped Cola's shoulders and pulled her close to him. "Look, I'm not fucking playing with you! You need to tone it the fuck down. I need you around to take over the world with me."

Cola felt the adrenaline of passion. "I'm here for you, but can I ask you a question?"

"Yeah, what's up?"

"Why is your dick hard?"

Spaz stared down at his manhood, yearning for attention. For years he had been concealing the sexual desires he had for Cola. He always imagined himself having rough sex with her. "Oh shit, I'm trippin'. I don't know what I'm thinking." Before he could get another word out his mouth, Cola's tongue was caressing his.

The next day Spaz was sitting in his office with Martini watching his every move. He wore a white Giorgio Armani suit and shoes. He sat behind his desk glancing at Martini, who was now staring out the window at the view of the Delaware River.

"You know what you are? A weak ass nigga," said Martini.

"What?" Spaz wondered where those words had suddenly come from.

"You know you want to leave the game alone, but you're scared of what might happen to you," said Martini, lighting the fire to Spaz' fuse. "I knew I was right all along. Didn't I say I wouldn't be holding my breath? I'd be dead as death itself if I had. I don't think you'll ever leave this place to be honest. I don't even know why you let the words out of your mouth about us moving to Southern California. You probably wouldn't know what to do with yourself. Scary ass nigga!"

He glared at her. "I'm a fuckin' boss! I do what I want. These bitch niggas do what they can! I'm getting money and I'm still hungry! I'm not in it for the chump change; I'm in it for the long run! I got that Black Card money, that Kobe Bryant, Lebron James money! We winning!"

Martini had enough. "Okay, you got money. I get it. But what are you going to do with it, Donald Trump?"

"Spend it all on you," said Spaz, positioning her on his lap and giving her a passionate kiss.

Martini enjoyed the kiss until his phone began ringing for the hundredth time. "Damn, who the hell is that?" she asked, getting annoyed.

"Cola's crazy ass."

"You need to tell her to stop calling you all the time," said Martini, getting jealous. "It seems like she's always calling you, and most of the time it's about shit she can handle on her own."

"You tell her," he said, knowing she was too scared to do so. Cola was a wild maniac, and no one wanted problems with her, not even Martini.

"Don't make me have to check her ass."

"Yeah right! And you say I'm the scary one . . . Give me a kiss." They began to make out.

Later on that evening, Spaz and Martini shared a wonderful time at the Laugh-House Comedy Club in downtown Philadelphia. The place was packed with people.

Once back inside the car, Martini picked up Spaz's cell phone lying on the armrest and noticed ten missed calls from Cola. "Your 'ho called again."

"Who you talking 'bout now?"

"Cola's stupid ass. You must be fucking her because it's not that much business in the world."

"Can we enjoy one night without all the bullshit?"

"Yeah, if you tell my cousin to stop calling!" Martini chuckled. "My damn cousin though, Spaz? Please tell me you didn't. Out of all the people in the world, you fucked her?"

"I'm just going to ignore you," Spaz said, driving up the highway.

"Like always. That's nothing new. You know that's the lowest of the low, right Spaz? Some lines just shouldn't be crossed, but I guess you just don't give a fuck." A tear slipped down her face and she wiped it away.

"One day . . ." Martini mumbled something.

"What the fuck you saying over there? You talking shit about me under your breath?"

"Nope. All I said is one day . . ."

Stiletto was nude, riding on top of Spaz' love handle. Her pussy slid up and down, getting wetter with each thrust. Her hair was in a ponytail and her back was dripping with sweat. Spaz lay comfortable on his S. Klutz king-sized mattress covered with expensive quilts and silk sheets. "Ooh, daddy, this feel so good," she said on the verge of an orgasm. No matter what Spaz did wrong, she always forgave him because the sex was so good she couldn't see herself with anyone else but him.

After spreading Stiletto's legs apart and pumping himself into multiple orgasms, Spaz fell into a deep sleep. Stiletto lay beside him staring at his facial features. She dreamed of having a child by the man she loved.

Spaz's cell phone began ringing, and then he received a text message. Stiletto picked up the phone and read the message.

Wow! Really? Let the phone ring three times and no answer. I don't have time to play with your disrespectful ass. Just let me know whazup because I want some of that dick.

Stiletto's anger detonated inside her body, filling her with pain.

She hovered over Spaz while he lay fast asleep snoring with his mouth wide open. She hated being lied to. *I should smother this nigga!* An outburst inside her body exploded in violence. Her hand landed viciously across Spaz' face, knocking him out of his sleep.

"Fuck!" Spaz yelled, watching Stiletto storm out the door. "Baby, wait!"

"I'm a kill this bitch!" said Stiletto, driving up the expressway in a rage. Her lips moved, but no words came out. Too many texts, phone calls, and pop up visits from Cola to Spaz raced through Stiletto's mind as she pieced it all together. This last text sent her over the edge. Cola knew damn well that Stiletto was dating Spaz. They'd spoken many times. When she ran through a red light she didn't feel any remorse. She was dressed in running sneakers, sweat pants, and a T-shirt. "This bitch is out of her mind," she said, parking in front of Cola's condo in the Germantown section of Philadelphia. She didn't bother to let Cola know she was on her way over because then she would have been on alert.

She exited the Lexus and strolled toward the front door of Cola's place. Stiletto rang the doorbell until Cola came to the door, half asleep. "What the hell you want?" said Cola.

"Spaz told me to come talk to you," she lied.

"Tell Spaz I said stop sending motherfuckers to my house." She slammed the door in Stiletto's face.

Stiletto, knocked again. *Really?* "Cola, open the door," she said, getting fed up with her disrespect.

"You want to talk? Come on in," she said, opening the door and welcoming Stiletto inside her home. "I'm grumpy this early in the morning, so you got to excuse me." Cola walked into the kitchen.

"It's all right, girl," she said, following her to the refrigerator. Cola grabbed a Corona and opened it with a bottle opener. "Help yourself, bitch. I don't serve no 'hos."

Who the fuck you calling a 'ho! "Anyway, I'll pass on the drink. I just wanted to talk to you," she said, following Cola to the kitchen.

"Well, what? Speak your mind then, shit. This is my relax day. I'm not trying to spend my entire day chitchatting with you."

"Okay, well, nice to see you in a good mood."

"Anyways."

"All I wanted to talk to you about is my man."

"Your man?"

"Yes, my man. You need to get off his dick."

Cola grew animated, moving her arms from side to side. "Bitch, you not even from our hood."

Stiletto's reflex was like a cat watching a housefly.

"You got blessed into the Black Boss Family. I'm queen bitch around here. Ump!" She cracked Stiletto in the head with the Corona bottle. "Bitch, you must be crazy!"

Stiletto fell to the ground. Her head was aching badly, blood dripped down her face. "I'm a fuck you up, bitch!" Stiletto promised. Her body was woozy.

Cola pushed the volume up on her radio to block out Stiletto's screams.

The Lox's tune called, "Fuck You," exploded through the speakers as Stiletto crawled around for her life.

"Mm!" Cola kicked Stiletto in the ribs and smacked her again with the Corona bottle, this time cracking it into a sharp weapon. Stiletto's weave was now bloody. "You come to my house talking shit to me? Mm!" She began stabbing Stiletto in the chest.

Cola felt the adrenaline pumping through her veins. Seeing Stiletto squirm made her feel tremendous. She stood over her to take her life as she struggled to breathe. "You don't have nothing to say now, huh, bitch?"

"Yeah, fuck you!" The horrifying shots from Stiletto's chrome .380 came ripping through Cola's chest, slamming her up against the wall.

No this bitch didn't just shoot me. She collapsed to the ground. Stiletto's blood was all over the floor, sofa, and walls. She looked down at her stomach to a grossing discovery. A huge chunk of her flesh was hanging.

"Ah! I got to get up." Stiletto stumbled to her feet, and a pounding headache attacked her. "Oh, my fucking head!" She stumbled to the kitchen and began opening drawers. BIG's "Suicidal Thoughts" thundered through the speakers.

Stiletto pulled a roll of duct tape from the kitchen drawers and stumbled past Cola's dead body. She made her way to the bathroom and set her gun on the sink just to the right of her.

Inside the bathroom she searched until she found some wet-wipes, and she began taping her wounds with them. "Ouu!" she screamed in tremendous pain. Stiletto took deep breaths as she contemplated her next move.

Cola lay bloody on the kitchen floor with her eyes closed. Her heart was still beating. She opened her eyes! The rage in her soul gave her the energy to rise to her feet. She heard water running from the bathroom sink and stumbled to the kitchen counter and clutched a steak knife.

Stiletto stood in the bathroom looking in the mirror. She washed the blood off her face and cut off the water. The hair on the back of her neck prickled. "Mmph!" Cola screamed, aiming the knife at Stiletto's neck, but it landed deeply in her shoulder.

"Ah!" Stiletto screamed out in pain. She elbowed Cola to the ground and aimed her gun. Cola was bleeding through her wounds, and she was close to death. She coughed repeatedly and screamed, "Fuck you!" She stumbled to the living room and saw Cola still breathing.

"You should have kept your big mouth closed," Stiletto said, putting a bullet in Cola's head. "Crazy bitch." The bullet slammed in Cola's skull, splattering her forehead.

Stiletto limped toward the front door. *I'm going to jail. Oh my god. I gotta dust my fingerprints.* Stiletto picked up a washcloth and started dusting areas she touched. *Look at all my blood on the floor. The cops going to know I killed her!* Stiletto cried and headed out the front door.

She made it out of Cola's house badly wounded and climbed inside her coupe. "Oh my god!" she cried, driving up to the intersection until she reached the Amoco gas station on Seventy-second and Ogontz. *Shit!* Stiletto winced in pain and parked on the side of pump number seven and exited the driver side. Once she slid her credit card in the machine and punched in her pin number, she raced to her trunk and grabbed the gas can. Stiletto filled it to the top and yelled, "Oh my god! Oh my god!" as she put the gas can in the backseat. She jumped in the car and drove out of the gas station and up Ogontz Avenue. *My chest is killing me.* Stiletto massaged her wounds with her hand. "Argh," she groaned.

She arrived back in Cola's driveway and took the keys out of the ignition. *Okay, you can do this.* She took a deep breath and exited the car.

Stiletto entered Cola's home with gas can in hand. *God, please help me out of this situation.* Tears raced down her face. Her body shook from pain and fear. She stood over Cola's dead body and began pouring gasoline, saturating her skin and her clothes. Pouring the rest of the fuel on the furniture, she then threw the gas can on the floor. She reached in her pocket and lit a piece of paper. Flames appeared and she dropped it on Cola's gasoline-soaked body. The fire burst around the dead corpse and the furniture.

Spaz tossed and turned from the sound of Stiletto crying at the edge of the bed. "Go back to sleep, baby. I'm tired," he said, irritated from the rude interruption.

Stiletto cried louder, waking Spaz completely.

"What the hell is wrong with you?" he asked, stretching in his silk sheets. "What the fuck?" he said, noticing blood soaking through her shirt. He sat up on the bed. "You bleeding."

"I know," she responded in tears.

"Oh shit! Who did this to you?" he asked, lifting her shirt and seeing the bootleg bandages on her chest.

"Cola," she answered in pain.

"I'm a kill that bitch!" he responded, picking up his phone.

Stiletto snatched the phone out his hand. "No, don't do that."

"Why not?" Spaz asked.

"I took care of it."

"You what?" he asked, rising to his feet.

"She's gone," she cried.

"What the fuck happened?" He paced the hardwood floors. "Matter fact, explain later. We got to get you to the hospital."

"No, no, I can't go to no hospital." Stiletto felt light-headed.

"Why not? Where is Cola?"

"She tried to kill me," she replied. "So I shot her."

"Aww man, are you fuckin' kidding me?"

Stiletto continued to cry. "I didn't know what else to do."

Spaz held her in his arms. *Man, this shit is crazy.* "Don't worry 'bout nothing. I got you, baby. Don't mention this to nobody, you understand?"

Stiletto nodded, "Yes."

"Let me call a private doctor," said Spaz, observing her wounds. "You will be all right. You definitely going to need some stitches." Spaz stared into her eyes. "Listen to me. Did you leave any evidence at the scene?"

"I lit the place on fire."

This girl is a rider. "Okay, good, good. Nobody going to know about this but me and you."

"They're going to kill me," she cried, referring to Grams.

"Nobody's going to hurt you, okay? You just keep your mouth closed."

"I swear it was self-defense, Spaz."

"Shhh," said Spaz. "Just be quiet. I got this." *How the fuck am I going to explain this? She did me a fucking favor anyway.*

Chapter Twenty-four
HEARTS OF FIRE

"Your sorry ass daddy not picking up the phone again," Martii said, once her call went to voice mail. "I hate him!" She sat in the condo that Spaz bought for her holding their one-year-old baby boy Yasmeen. Martini thought of many incidents of his cheating and disloyalty. She learned his personality and movements, so she was able to date on the side without getting caught, but she was starting to get a little careless.

"Damn, ma, when are you going to leave Spaz?" her secret boo asked her in a frustrated tone.

"Boy, please! You know he will kill both of us."

"I'm not scared of dude."

"Ronny, please stop talking like that. You are an NBA basketball player, not a gangster."

"Look, I have loved you since high school. I was your first love. We belong together. Always have."

Martini began to get wet thinking of the first time she had sex with Ronny. "That was a long time ago, but it seems like yesterday."

"I know, baby. When I first got drafted to the Lakers I was pissed off when you didn't move with me to California."

"You know Spaz wouldn't let me leave, boo."

"Yeah, I know, but you should have left anyway."

Martini thought of leaving Philadelphia, but she was too scared.

"The primary reason for the move back to Philly was to be with you, and you still won't move in with me. Playing with the 76ers wasn't my dream, baby. But I forced a trade just so I could be with you. That should tell your ass a lot."

"It does. But it's not that easy, Ronny!"

"Of course it's not. You love Spaz."

"But I don't even know if I want to be with him anymore."

"What about the baby? How could you tell that man that my child is his when you know in your heart he is my son?"

Martini's eyes watered from guilt. "You just do not understand, Ronny. Spaz is a murderer. He will have me killed if he found out that I have been lying to him. I am afraid for my life. I don't want to think about what could happen." Martini started to cry hysterically.

"Calm down, baby girl. We will figure some way out of this drama."

"Can you promise me that you will do whatever needs to be done to rectify this situation?"

"I promise," Ronny said.

Spaz entered the bedroom scaring Martini half to death. "Who the fuck is you talking to?"

Martini's heart dropped, but she responded quickly. "My mother, boy, and why are you cursing? By the way, Spaz, she heard you. Bye, Mom, I will call you back later."

Spaz yelled out, "Sorry, Mrs. Jenkins."

Martini hung up the phone. "She said don't make her come over here and put you in your place."

Spaz burst into laughter. He relaxed beside her in the bed, flirting with Martini's thick frame. Spaz slowly removed her lingerie while kissing her body all over. He pushed his jeans to the floor and entered her wet pussy, and pumped in and out until sperm squirted from his love muscle.

After the passionate sex session, Martini rested on her cozy bed with a thousand thoughts racing through her head.

Spaz noticed the tears on her face. "What are you crying for?"

Martini remained silent.

"What's wrong?"

Martini rose to her feet and ran to the living room.

Spaz followed behind. "Yo, what is up with you, girl?"

Their conversation was interrupted by the doorbell. Martini walked to the living room to open the door. She noticed an attractive young female through the peephole, so she opened the door. "May I help you?"

"Hello, I didn't mean to bother you, but I just moved in next door and I was hanging some paintings on the walls and realized that I could complete the job faster if I had a nail gun. I was hoping I could borrow one from you. You know it's hard to get help from a good man these days, so I have to do it myself."

Spaz heard the familiar voice and walked to the living room. His heart fell to the floor. Stiletto stood by the front door.

"Don't worry, we have one and you are welcome to borrow it. Let me get it for you." Martini disappeared to the back closet to look for the nail gun.

Spaz looked in Stiletto's eyes and spoke in a low, angry tone. "What the fuck are you doing here?"

Stiletto smiled. "I followed your lying ass. So this is why you hide your feelings from me? This must be why you don't love me, Spaz."

Spaz put his finger in her face. "Yo, you trippin'."

"You lying piece of shit!" Stiletto had enough, and she swung a hard punch to his chest. "I'm a teach you not to play with me," she said in a low voice.

Martini emerged from the hallway with a nail gun. "Here it is. You can keep it until you are done with it. I don't think we will need it for a while."

"Thank you! You are so kind for allowing me to borrow this." Stiletto pressed the nail gun to Spaz's forehead and pulled the trigger. The three-inch nail drilled through Spaz' skull, and he collapsed to the ground.

Martini screamed. Stiletto reached inside her Coach bag and pulled out a small pistol. Martini kept screaming until a bullet inside her right eye silenced her. Her body hit the floor, and Stiletto crept away leaving the two to die a bloody death.

Stiletto snapped out of her daydream. She was so pissed off at Spaz, but she played it cool.

"By the way, my name is Stiletto, and I have been fucking your man," she said, walking back to her car.

Martini's jaw dropped. "Excuse me, bitch?"

Stiletto paused. "Oh, I got your bitch," she said, pulling out her .38 snub nose from her Coach bag.

"Spaz, do something!" Martini screamed as she held her hands up and slowly backed away.

Spaz backed away from the door and then slammed it.

This bitch is crazy! Spaz stared out the window at Stiletto, who took aim at his GT Bentley parked out front. She pulled the trigger and shots rang out, shattering his windows and leaving bullet holes on the passenger door.

She threw the nail gun to the street and headed for her Lexus. "You can't have your cake and eat it too, motherfucker! I'm that crazy bitch your mother warned you about," she said and pressed her foot on the gas pedal.

Stiletto drove her Lexus at eighty miles an hour with the radio on silent, replaying in her head the times she shared with Spaz. She recalled asking him if he had a woman that he loved and what his responses were. Did that mean that he was a liar? Did the woman he lived with have his heart, and was he in denial? Was he playing games with her feelings? Was Spaz a womanizer? All these thoughts racing through her mind caused her to swerve in the far left lane of the freeway. Her phone rang loudly and distracted her mental state. She screamed, "Leave me alone. I don't feel like being bothered!" As she screamed those words her conscious state began to change. Was she losing control? She wiped her eyes and smiled. "Fuck it! He wants to play games with me, let's see how he likes this shit that I am going to do to him."

Stiletto spent a nice penny at the mall on several high-end shoes, all at Spaz' expense. Although she knew the $8,000 wouldn't put a dent in his pockets, she felt much better. She drove the rest of the way home listening to Anita Baker's "Caught up in the Rapture" on repeat.

Once she got home, she pushed the door open to her lonely apartment. As she placed her bags down on the soft white living room carpet, she felt a cool breeze coming from her bedroom. She pulled out the .38 caliber that Spaz had given her and tiptoed to her bedroom with the thought of someone robbing her. Lurking in the narrow hallway, Stiletto pushed open her bedroom door completely and walked in with the gun in her hand. The curtain moved back and forth from a breeze pushing through the window. "I thought I closed that window when I left," she said to herself, putting her pistol back in her purse and closing the window. Suddenly she felt a tight grip around her neck. She struggled to get her balance and noticed the masked man wore leather gloves. He pressed them against her mouth.

She struggled to scream as the gunman whispered in her ear, "I am going to kill you, bitch. But before I do, I am going to get me some of your luscious pussy." The masked man slammed her to the bed and took his mask off.

Stiletto was scared to death until the man revealed his face. Although her heart was broken, she was happy to see him. "Spaz, why the fuck did you scare me like that? I can't stand your ass!"

Spaz laughed aloud. "Damn, girl, you was scared as shit. Your heart is beating fast as hell. Stop shaking, baby. I was just fucking with you."

The hard stare Stiletto gave him was meant to give her time to assess her situation with him. She felt like Spaz was playing a game with her. She could not hold back the rage any longer. She rose off the bed and swung as hard as she could, and slapped Spaz in the face. Knocked that smile right off his face.

Spaz's head jerked back as he grabbed his face. "Bitch, what the fuck is wrong with you? Are you crazy?"

"No, I am not crazy. I am wounded. I can't believe you hurt me like that. You said you would never do this to me. How could you break your promise to me?"

"Hold up. You just slapped me, didn't you?" Spaz slammed Stiletto back down to the bed as Stiletto pulled out her pistol and aimed it at him.

"Get the fuck off me, Spaz!"

Spaz grew puzzled. "You slapped me and pulled a gun out on me? I love you, girl. Give me that gun!" Spaz snatched the gun out of her hand and grabbed her close. "Boo, I apologize. I didn't tell you about my baby-mom because we are on the verge of breaking up."

"Baby-mom? Oh, hell naw." Stiletto pushed him off her.

"I don't love her no more. I'm tryna fuck with you. You see I didn't trip about you coming over to the crib, right? I have developed feelings for you, Stiletto. I'm falling in love with you."

That four letter word melted in Stiletto's heart. The words she had been waiting for were finally said but . . . She wanted to believe him since she cared for Spaz deeply. "You are lying, Spaz. You will say anything right now."

"I mean it, baby. You are so fly. I like your style, and I enjoy making love to you." Spaz gave her a soft, wet kiss. His tongue massaged hers. Spaz laid her on the bed and began to pull off her leggings.

Stiletto spoke softly. "I'm mad at you, Spaz."

Spaz stuck his head between her soft thighs and began licking and fingering her wet vagina. Stiletto moaned softly. Each minute felt more heavenly than the other. She felt her vagina overflowing with juices from this pleasurable moment of being tongue massaged by the man she loved. Spaz licked her clit and squeezed her ass so passionately that she exploded in pleasurable harmony. He crawled his way to her glossy lips and kissed her softly. "You know you're initiated into the Black Boss Family."

"What?"

"Welcome to my organization. I've got some hits to do tomorrow at a pool hall. You rolling with me or what?" he asked Stiletto.

"Damn, you know how to fuck up a romantic evening," Stiletto said, turning away from him.

"This is my world. You're either for me or against me. Which is it?"

Stiletto turned toward him. "I guess you'll find out in the morning."

Chapter Twenty-five
MURDER FEST

Grams tried to talk Spaz out of attending the murder fest, but Spaz had his mind made up. Grams enjoyed getting paid for murders. He cocked the hammer back and headed inside the pool hall. Spaz and Stiletto headed in behind them, strapped, side by side. Slugger exited the car and headed into the pool hall.

The cashier was an older Italian cat in his mid-forties. His eyes followed Spaz as he placed a twenty-dollar bill on the counter. The cashier took the money and gave Spaz his change.

Spaz said, "Rack 'em up, motherfucker!"

Stiletto grabbed the pool stick as Spaz placed the balls in order.

Two couples playing pool decided to exit the pool hall after recognizing the Black Boss Family. Grams looked down at his watch and grew impatient. The pool hall was empty except Spaz and his team. The cashier's eyes followed Spaz like a hawk.

Stiletto hit the cue ball, cracking the rack, and two colored balls went into separate pockets. "Yes!"

Spaz looked down at his watch. *What the fuck is taking these cats so long*? Grams couldn't stand still from the anticipation of murder.

Slugger remained calm as always. He knew everything was going to go down according to plan.

The cashier's evil eyes were as quick as lightning. As Spaz grabbed the stick and aimed at the white ball, the cashier ducked behind the counter and came up with a twelve shot automatic shotgun. His aim was on Spaz's chest. The explosive buckshot attacked Spaz, catching him in the chest, and violently knocking him to the ground. Stiletto screamed as she pulled out her .45 caliber and returned fire. The first two shots barely missed him as he took shelter behind the counter.

The Polo brothers emerged from the back of the pool hall holding AK's with silencers and hundred round drums. Their aim was at Grams and Slugger. Multiple shots came so quick that they barely got a chance to pull their guns out and get a good aim at the Polo brothers.

Slugger fell hard to the ground. "Shit, I'm hit!" he said, feeling the sharp pain in his leg.

Grams took cover and started firing back. "You all right?" he yelled to Slugger.

"Yeah, it went in and out." Slugger took cover under the pool table.

Bullets from Grams' gun caught the Polo brothers by surprise. Their attention was so focused on Stiletto with the thought of the cashier blazing Spaz, that they underestimated the quickness of the trigger. One single shot exploded one of the brother's head. Skull fragments and blood splattered, as the other brother caught a stray shot in the eye socket and shoulder.

Grams celebrated his bull's-eye. "Now I can see what you're thinking, motherfucker!"

The Polo brothers lay slumped on the bloody pool tables. Spaz lay unconscious under the pool table. Stiletto continued screaming while firing at the cashier. The cashier rose to his feet with his pump. Stiletto ducked behind the pool table, and the shot almost took her head off. Grams and Slugger began firing at the cashier as he ducked behind the counter. Bullets tore the counter apart. Blood dripped from Spaz's mouth as Stiletto held him.

"Don't die, baby. Please don't die. I love you, Spaz."

Grams noticed a reflection of the cashier through the mirror that hung from the ceiling. He signaled to Slugger. As soon as the cashier rose to his feet to bust more shots, a shot caught him in the hand and shoulder. The cashier fell to the ground, dropping his pump to the floor.

Slugger signaled and Grams moved in. The cashier stumbled to his feet after getting knocked to the floor from gunshots. His weapon lay on the floor as he tried desperately to grasp it.

Grams had him at point-blank range. "Pussy, don't move!" Grams yelled as he began to pistol whip the cashier.

Slugger picked up the cashier's shotgun. Stiletto catered to Spaz, who struggled to breathe, while bleeding from the mouth. She rose to her feet after seeing the cashier get hit. Stiletto ran toward the cashier, screaming with her gun aimed at his head. She pulled the trigger. One bullet barely missed his head and the other caught him in the shoulder.

Grams stopped Stiletto from killing him. "Chill, baby girl. We going to torture this motherfucker. Slugger, you go get the car. Stiletto, you help Spaz to his feet while I put this piece of shit in the trunk."

Slugger ran to the whip and backed it up to the entrance and hopped back out. He and Stiletto helped carry Spaz to the car. Then Slugger made it back to Grams and the cashier.

Grams smacked the cashier once more, knocking him unconscious. "You bitch-ass nigga! Yo, open the trunk and help me carry this fat motherfucker!"

Slugger and Grams lifted the Italian gunman and slammed him into the trunk.

During the ride to the hospital, Stiletto cried her eyes out. "Don't die, baby! Don't die!"

Grams swallowed his anger while pulling up to Saint Jersey Hospital in Camden, New Jersey. The long ride was necessary to escape the jurisdiction of the incident and avoid police questioning. "Stiletto, take him inside, and you can catch a cab home. Remember to tell the hospital staff that someone robbed you two and shot Spaz."

Paramedics escorted Spaz to the emergency room while Stiletto followed, with a face full of tears.

The cashier still lay conscious but was in total darkness. He struggled to move. His vision slowly returned, and he found himself tied to a metal chair. "Help!"

Grams and Slugger emerged from behind the door. "Don't start bitching now. You shot my man and he might die, so I don't give a fuck about you or your tears. Now tell me who sent you to kill us?"

The cashier remained silent. Grams smacked him in the head with the pistol, splitting his forehead.

"Shit! Kill me, motherfucker! I'm not telling you shit!"

Grams looked surprised.

Slugger smacked him with the pistol, bloodying his face even more.

"Oh, we got a tough guy, Slugger. This motherfucker thinks he built like that."

"Fuck you, nigger. That's why I fucked your mother!"

Slugger aimed his gun to his head and Grams stopped him.

"Don't shoot him. That's what he wants. He wants us to take him out of his misery, but I got a better idea." Grams walked to the back door that led to the yard and opened it. "Come here, boy." A huge, full-blooded, 200 pound pit bull came running from its doghouse. Grams had raised the beast since he was a pup. "Hey, boy, we got us a little problem." Grams connected a thick chain to his spiked collar. "Come on, boy." Grams walked the dog in front of the cashier.

His heart dropped to his knees. "Oh my God! Help me," he prayed.

Grams frowned. "Now, I'm going to ask you one more time, motherfucker. Who told you to kill us?"

"I don't know what you're talking about!"

"Get him, boy!"

The pit attacked the cashier, biting a huge piece of flesh from his leg. Blood dripped from the pit bull's mouth.

"Come on. Please just kill me. I don't know what you're talking about!"

Grams grew angry that the cashier was lying. "Get him, boy!"

The pit bull attacked again and bit large bites of the cashier's thighs. The pit bull's head shook from side to side, tearing the skin and flesh from his body.

The cashier screamed in pain. "How can I tell you something I don't know?"

Grams grew furious. "You lying motherfucker. Get him, boy!"

The pit jumped into the cashier's lap, looking him face to face as he snarled. The pit bull was so close to the cashier's face that he could smell the dog food on his breath. The pit bull took bites of his cheek and face.

Slugger turned his head, avoiding the gruesome sight. Flesh and blood tore from the cashier's face as he screamed at the top of his lungs. "Okay, okay, I will tell you. Please get this dog off of me!"

Grams chuckled with a mischievous look in his eyes. "Good boy." The huge dog had blood smeared on his face. Grams took him back to the yard and closed the door.

Slugger had seen Grams kill before. But never had he seen him this angry. *Goddamn, this nigga is enjoying this shit.*

"Will you tell us what we need to know before this fuckin' dog eats you alive?"

"Okay, please don't call that damn dog back, please. Listen, I will tell you everything if you promise to put a bullet in my head afterwards."

Grams cocked back his hammer. "I promise, motherfucka."

The cashier took a deep breath. "Listen, Sticky put the hit on Spaz!"

Slugger looked at Grams. "I told you!" Slugger turned his attention back to the cashier. "Why, motherfucker? Why does he want Spaz dead? Spaz was good to him."

The cashier struggled to talk from pain. "It has nothing to do with how good he has been to him. Sticky doesn't give a shit about that. It goes deeper than that."

Grams snapped. "Well, talk, motherfucker!"

"Okay, okay. Sticky is being watched closely by the Feds, and you know how these wise guys are. If you know too much, you might be the one getting whacked. Spaz is getting too powerful, and Sticky can't afford to lose his position."

Grams got frustrated. "Pussy, you are leaving shit out! I'm about to get my fucking dog again!"

"No! Let me finish. We rigged his father's home—the wiring and all . . . Flash—that was his name, right? Sticky also put a tail on the broad Pearl. The day the kid brought his father to the house and Pearl was there, was the day his parents took their last breaths."

Slugger and Grams glanced at each other.

"What! Why would he kill his family, you dumb fuck?"

"Do I have to spell it out for you? Sticky was sleeping with Spaz' mother, and he loved her. Sticky felt as if Pearl was busting his balls, so he tied them up and set the house on fire. The cameras never show anyone coming into the house because those were rigged too. That is it. Now please kill me, motherfucker!" The cashier kept yelling and screaming until a hollow point slug silenced him.

"Motherfucker!" Grams let off five more shots into his chest. "That's for Spaz, you stupid fuck!"

Chapter Twenty-six
ATTEMPTED MURDER

"You better not die on me, motherfucka," said Stiletto, pacing the floor of the hospital room with tears flowing from her eyes. She could not stop looking over at Spaz. Her anxiety grew. She was praying for any sudden change in his state as he lay motionless. "Baby, can you hear me? Are you okay?"

His only response was a slight movement of his right hand. She called in the nurse to check his vital signs and give her an update constantly on his breathing patterns.

The nurse said, "There is no change in his condition since my last update to you."

"Are you guys taking good care of him?" Stiletto reached over and kissed Spaz on his forehead. "I love you, Spaz. Don't stop fighting. This will be over soon. When this is over, we are going to celebrate."

As Spaz lay in the hospital bed, Stiletto kept having flashbacks of recent incidents. The guns shooting, the blood, the dead bodies, and the end result of this dark hospital room. "Why?" Stiletto asked herself. Her love for him and the possibility that he might not live stirred up her anger, and she kicked the bathroom door, slamming it closed.

The nurse frowned with disapproval. "Please calm down. Otherwise, I will have to ask you to leave the room."

"Are you crazy? I am not leaving my man alone. You better do all it takes to get him back to normal. We have plans for our lives." Stiletto began to cry again. "I love him so much. We're supposed to be together. He means so much to me—he's my life. You don't understand. He's gotta live. Please!"

The nurse interrupted her. "I know you love this man. I can tell from your actions, but I must tell you something that you need to know."

Stiletto moved closer to Spaz, and she felt his hand moving firmly.

The nurse continued, "He's lost a lot of blood, and because of that he will not be able to just get up and walk out of here.

A couple weeks after surgery, Spaz laid low in a huge New Jersey house he and Stiletto shared. Stiletto catered to his every need. Therapy took place at a private spot on the outskirts of Jersey where Spaz did stretch exercises and numerous Tae-Bo methods to make his mind, body, and soul stronger. All he could think about was his son after almost losing his life. He attempted to contact Martini several times, but never got an answer. He wanted to contact her badly, so he called Grams. "Yo, what's good?"

"Who is this? Spaz, is that you, nigga?"

"Yeah, you niggas thought I was dead. That's what I wanted everybody to think. I'm good though."

"Yo, man, we got something to tell you. It's important. We have to talk in person."

Spaz rubbed the hairs on his chin. "Meet me down Penn's Landing by the bridge at eight tonight.

"Yo, we'll be there."

"All right, I'll see you then."

Spaz knew that something big was about to happen.

At eight o'clock Stiletto pushed Spaz in his wheelchair. Both of them were strapped, ready for the unexpected.

Grams and Slugger awaited his arrival.

"Spaz, what's up, player?" Slugger and Grams gave their boss handshakes and hugs.

"Yo, my nigga. What the fuck! How long will you have to be in this nut-ass wheelchair?"

"Just for a minute. I should be out of this by next week."

"We glad you're alive. Me and Grams thought you were dead."

"I'm good. I will be dammed if I let them kill me. But I'm curious to know what information you have about the situation."

Slugger and Grams glanced at each other, unsure of which one should give the bad news to Spaz.

Grams grew impatient. "Look, Spaz, that Sticky is a fucking snake! He had you set up to be killed.

Spaz nodded his head no. "Naaah. I don't know about all that. Maybe the Polo brothers found out that we were going to kill them and struck first. I make Sticky a lot of money and it doesn't make sense for him to get rid of me."

Slugger cut in. "Me and Grams kidnapped one of them clowns, and we tortured him. He told us that Sticky put the hit out on you."

"Why would Sticky want to kill me?" Spaz was in denial.

Grams took a deep breath. "Listen Spaz, I had my dog damn near chew this motherfucker's face off, and he started singing like a bird."

There was a long pause, and then Slugger said, "He also had your parents killed."

"What the fuck did you just say?" Spaz's blood pressure shot up as he glared at Slugger.

Grams sighed. "It's true, man. When your father came home, your mom kicked Sticky to the curb. Sticky flipped out and killed both of them but made it seem like a bad wiring accident."

Spaz balled his fists. "I am going to kill that motherfucker!" he said, feeling the pain in his chest from the outburst.

"Spaz, let us handle it for you."

"No, this situation is personal. Give me some time to heal, and that motherfucker is dead."

Slugger agreed. "Okay, we got your back. Don't make any moves without us."

"A'ight, I'm out." Spaz's heart grew numb from betrayal. He couldn't believe Sticky would do this to him.

Stiletto remained silent and assisted Spaz back to the passenger seat of the Range Rover.

Spaz sat on the passenger side while Stiletto drove. He didn't want to be spotted.

She glanced at Spaz. "I am glad you're feeling better, baby."

Spaz began shadow boxing. "I still got it. I am still here. Now, let's go handle this gangster shit."

Agent Mark Rizzo was sitting on a beach in Florida. "I needed this vacation." He chatted to his wife about retiring.

Mark Rizzo was one of the hardest working federal agents on the job. The investigations and the court cases were beginning to take a toll on him and his family. His wife often begged him to retire.

"Baby, I'm working on a big case. I promise after this one I'm retiring."

To his wife those words were starting to sound like a broken record. It was hard to enjoy his vacation with work on his mind. Sticky was going to be his bread and butter. Once Sticky went down, he figured the rest would fall into place.

Sticky and his gunman were relaxing at the Tops-Up Lounge. It was a beautiful day, so they were enjoying the weather while sitting at an umbrella table. Sticky was sipping on coffee.

Traffic cruised up the one-way street in front of Tops-Up Lounge. A red F-150 truck pulled up in front of Sticky and his gunman. A young African American female with long blonde hair-weave and black shades honked the horn to get Sticky's attention. Sticky placed his attention on the beautiful-looking woman. He was always fascinated with beautiful black women. He lusted off her features.

She poked her head out of the driver's window. "Excuse me, sir. Do you know which way Broad Street is?"

Sticky's mouth watered as he envisioned her going down on him. She looked a little familiar, but he was unsure. "Yeah, go straight down to the red light and make a right-hand turn and the next block will be Broad Street."

Within seconds, three black masked men emerged from the back of the pickup truck aiming AK-47s at Sticky and his gunman. Loud shots turned the quiet block into a noisy explosion. Bullets showered the area as tables flipped and windows shattered. Sticky reached for his gun but was stopped by numerous bullets hitting his chest. The bullets caused him to flip over the chair and onto the concrete. His gunman managed to get a couple shots off, but three bullets to his face sent him to his death.

Sticky lay on his back in total darkness. His chest burned from the pain. All he could see were clouds, and he thanked God for letting him survive. Suddenly a Timberland boot pressed down on his chest, and one of the masked men looked down on him with an AK-47 pointed at his head. Sticky's heart dropped as he looked down the eye of the barrel.

The masked man took a deep breath. "This is for my mom and dad, motherfucker!"

After hearing those words, Sticky knew exactly who the masked man was. "Spaz, don't do this, kid. Don't do this." Sticky barely got his words out as blood gushed from his mouth.

Spaz's tears soaked through the black mask. "You tried to kill me, motherfucker, and I am still here. Now it's your turn to die!" Spaz squeezed the trigger. Long flames exited the barrow. The shots tore Sticky's head from his neck. Blood squirted on Spaz's black outfit.

Stiletto yelled from the F-150 pickup truck, "Yo, come the fuck on. The cops are coming!"

Spaz ignored her words, and he let off more rounds into Sticky's chest.

"Yo, come on, man. You're going to get us locked up!" Grams shook his head.

Spaz raced back to the truck and climbed in the back. Stiletto pulled off, burning rubber as she raced through red lights. *Where the hell was Nikki Montagna? I know he'll be coming for me*, Spaz thought.

Chapter Twenty-seven
LETHAL INVESTIGATION

Mark Rizzo arrived back to the city from his vacation. His fellow agents gave him the news about Sticky Scilionni and his heart dropped. With Sticky dead, his plans were ruined.

"Goddamn!" All the work he did, all the evidence he had on Sticky Scilionni was a waste of time. "I had that cocksucker in the palm of my hands." Rizzo grew depressed as he sat in his living room. He flicked through stations as the six clock news was being broadcast.

"Earlier this evening, mob boss, Sticky Scilionni, and his gunman Bobby Corleone were gunned down outside of Tops-Up Lounge. Police have no suspects. It's been a blood bath across the city. The total murders so far are 455, and there are still two months left in the year. This year has been a record high for murders."

Agent Rizzo shut the TV off and threw the remote up against the wall. He then raced down to the office and made a few calls requesting the cameras that they planted in front of Tops-Up Lounge.

Mark Rizzo received the tapes he requested and began watching. The tape showed Sticky and his gunman drinking coffee while discussing business. Agent Rizzo snapped, "All the money we get from the government and this is the best audio we can get?"

Agent Danny Chambers adjusted the audio on a mixing board. "Now that's better."

The tape showed a red F-150 pull up. The agent's eyes grew wide in suspense. Stiletto wore a blonde wig and glasses, so it was hard for the detectives to identify her. Three men jumped out the back of the pickup truck wearing black masks, which made it difficult to identify them as well.

Rizzo spent days trying to put the puzzle together. He was determined to build this case. His wife pleaded with him to retire, but it was like talking to a brick wall.

Spaz was extremely nervous, knowing that if the mob had a clue that he killed Sticky, he and his whole family would be dead. His heart raced rapidly as he headed into the funeral wearing a black Louis Vuitton suit and black gator shoes.

Sticky lay in his casket, stiff and peaceful. Spaz looked down on his corpse pretending to be upset about the loss of his boss. For a moment he felt Sticky's presence and jumped from the sight of Sticky's eyes opening. His mind was playing tricks on him. He placed a hollow point AK-bullet in his casket, remembering the day he killed Sticky with the AK-47. He began to remember the deaths of his mother and father and could visualize Sticky killing them both out of jealousy. Tears burst from his eyes, making his sympathy for the dead seem realistic. Stiletto wrapped her arms around him as he and his entourage headed out the door.

Spaz made it outside of the church. His men followed. He kept his eyes on the passenger side of his SUV. He then heard a familiar voice calling his name and turned around. Nikki Montagna was standing behind him with two of his men. Spaz' heart dropped. He imagined Nikki Montagna pulling out a gun and shooting him in the face.

Spaz swallowed his nerves and said, "I'm sorry about what happened to Sticky. Did any word get back on who did this?"

Nikki Montagna remained silent for a few seconds, and then decided to ignore the statement Spaz made. "You were a good asset to our business. You made Sticky a richer man. He supplied you, and I'm going to take his place. I want the same respect you gave him, and I'll give you the same product at the same price."

Spaz held back the joy he felt about keeping his business going. "Of course, I'm a good businessman. I plan to keep everybody happy. You get yourself together, and when you are ready for the next shipments, call me."

The two hugged and went their separate ways. Spaz sat in his truck and sighed in relief. He then wiped the sweat from his forehead.

After the funeral, memories raced through Spaz' head. Tears always seemed to fall from his eyes whenever he came to the graveyard to visit his parents. "I love y'all, and I want you both to know that you can rest in peace now because I took care of your killer."

Spaz drove up the street and made several attempts to get in contact with Martini to see his son. Spaz began to get worried, wondering if Sticky sent his men to kill Martini and his son. Every time his phone rang his heart would get a tingle, thinking it could be kidnappers calling for ransom money. Spaz dialed Grams number and commanded him to find his baby's mother and his son.

Martini and Ronny pulled up at Martini's little sister's house inside of a dark colored Suburban. Martini looked deep into Ronny's eyes and gave him a kiss. "I love you, boo."

Ronny nervously handed her the baby. "All right, little man. I will see you later."

Martini grabbed Yasmeen and headed to the front door. Her little sister, Stephanie, raced to the door.

"Yasmeen! Hey, little cutie." Stephanie looked up to her big sister and followed her every move. She was seventeen going on thirty.

Martini always let Stephanie babysit when she wanted to go out. "Here, girl, take this hundred dollars." Martini reached in her purse and fished out the money." This should be more than enough to last you through the weekend."

Stephanie smiled. "Don't worry, me and my nephew are going to be all right. We gone have some fun."

Martini kissed Yasmeen. "Behave yourself. Don't be crying all the time." She gave him another kiss and headed back to the car. "Stephanie, make sure you take good care of my baby."

"I will. Don't worry about anything, just call me later."

Martini got back in the car and headed up the road. Ronny stared out the window on the passenger side. "Man, I am tired of all this hiding shit."

Martini rolled her eyes. "What are you talking about now, Ronny?"

"I am talking about all this ducking and hiding. I am tired of this shit. I want to go out somewhere."

"I already told you, you're a basketball star now, and I don't want to get caught in too many pictures of us together. Spaz would go crazy."

"Well, I am hungry. Let's stop and get something to eat."

Martini frowned. "Okay! Okay!"

The Burger King drive-thru was crowded. Martini and Ronny waited in the long line. Finally, Martini pulled up to the drive-through window, placed her order, and pulled up to the window to pay. She received the food and pulled off into traffic. "Are you happy now?"

"I can't even remember the last time I ate at Burger King. You nervous, baby?"

"A lot. I just hope everything turns out right for us."

In the car behind Ronny and Martini were Grams and Slugger. Grams eyebrows rose. "There go that bitch right there!"

Slugger watched closely. "Hold on, don't jump to conclusions."

"What the fuck you mean 'don't jump to conclusions'? This bitch is in the car with another nigga!" Grams pointed.

"Man, you don't know who that is. That could be her brother or her cousin."

Grams shook his head in disagreement.

They continued to follow them to a condo with a few nice cars parked in the garage. Ronny exited the car quickly and dashed around to the driver's side and opened the door for Martini.

Martini exited the car with a huge smile on her face. "Aww, baby, you haven't opened the door for me since high school." Then they gave each other a juicy kiss.

Grams angrily looked at Slugger. "Motherfucker, do siblings or cousins kiss like that?"

Slugger shook his head, knowing Grams was right.

Martini and Ronny headed toward the front door holding hands and entered the home. Slugger watched closely as Grams wrote the address down.

"Spaz is going to be upset when I tell him this shit." Grams put the car in drive and headed up the road.

Chapter Twenty-eight
UNNECESSARY MAYHEM

"I wish Spaz would stop calling me. Damn, can't he get the hint?" Martini and Ronny rose from their bed.

"Baby, don't let him get you upset. We are leaving here tonight."

"Yeah, baby, you right. Let's go get Yasmeen and get ready for our flight."

"Thank God for the contract to play basketball overseas away from all the bullshit. Everything is falling in place," said Ronny.

"Hey, big sis, so how was your weekend?" asked Stephanie, walking on the front porch holding her nephew.

"Good, girl. What about you? Did Yasmeen give you any problems?"

"No, my little nephew loves me. He drove Mommy crazy." She laughed. "I left him with her while I went to the store and when I got back he was crying at the top of his lungs."

Martini smiled as she held Yasmeen and headed toward the Suburban where Ronny was waiting in the driver's seat. Stephanie followed. Martini placed Yasmeen in the car seat. "Moesha, is everything all right?"

"Yeah, why would you ask that?" Martini covered her true thoughts. She couldn't explain to her sister that she and Ronny were running away together, so she lied.

"I don't know. You have been acting really strange."

Martini looked her sister in the eyes and hugged her. "I love you, Stephanie, and I got something to tell you . . . never mind." A tear rolled down Martini's cheek. She walked to the driver's seat feeling ashamed and guilty about her actions.

By the time they pulled into Ronny's parking lot, Martini was stressed out and a nervous wreck. "Come on, bay. Let's finish packing."

Ronny's house was small but cozy with plenty of love that breezed through the air. He laid the baby in the bedroom and tucked him in his crib. Martini reached in the refrigerator and grabbed some ground beef to prepare their last meal in the house. She felt a cold breeze and immediately looked at the kitchen window. It was half opened. Her heart tingled. "Ronny, I thought you said you closed and locked the windows before we left."

"I did," Ronny replied. *What the hell is this girl talking about?*

Martini noticed the plant by the window was knocked over. She thought about someone breaking into her house and robbing them but nothing was stolen. A leather-gloved hand covered her mouth and interrupted her thoughts. She tried to scream, but her scream was silenced by the tight grip around her mouth. Martini tried to get free, but the masked man had a tight grip on her mouth and waist.

Ronny made his way through the narrow hallway. The closet door flew open, striking him on the forehead. He fell to the ground, letting out a painful groan.

A masked man emerged from the closet with a chrome Desert Eagle in his hand. "Don't move, motherfucker!"

Ronny begged for his life. "Please don't shoot. Take anything you want. I have twenty thousand in my safe. Please don't kill us. My one-year-old son is in the bedroom sleep. Please don't kill us."

Spaz stared at Ronny through his mask. "What's your son's name?"

"Uh, his name is Yasmeen."

Grams pushed Martini into the living room as he gripped her tightly with his hand around her mouth. She bit his finger to let out a quick scream. "I know it's you, Spaz. Stop! Why are you doing this?"

Grams put her back in a tight grip.

"Go get my little man," said Spaz.

Slugger followed the order and brought the baby into the living room.

Ronny tried to reason. "Come on, man. Don't do this. I wanted to talk to you about this, but Martini wouldn't let me. I told her that it was wrong to blame a baby on you that's not yours."

Martini couldn't believe her ears. "You coward-ass nigga! Ronny, shut up. He is going to kill you!"

Spaz had enough of Martini interfering in their conversation. "Grams, tie her up and duct tape her loud mouth."

With no hesitation Grams pushed Martini to the floor and duct taped her mouth, hands, and legs.

Spaz glanced at Slugger holding Yasmeen. "Take the baby and wait for us in the car."

Ronny expressed pain and regret for the dishonesty. "Please don't hurt my son," Ronny cried.

Spaz took his mask off and stooped down to where Ronny lay in submission. "So let me get this right. You are saying that you're the father of that baby?"

Ronny answered yes.

Spaz smacked Ronny with the butt of the gun, sending him into total darkness. Minutes later, Ronny awoke with his and Martini's hands tied and their mouths duct taped. Grams and Spaz were pouring gasoline on their bodies. They tried to scream, but the duct tape over their mouths silenced their cries. They wiggled and squirmed, but there was no use. They were going to die.

Spaz noticed all the packed bags. "Damn, baby, you were just going to leave and not say goodbye? Now you know that's not right." Spaz lit a Dutch Master as a tear dropped down his eye. "How could you do this to me, Martini?"

She tried to respond but couldn't. Martini stared into Spaz' eyes, and she remembered why he looked so familiar the day they met. She flashed back to when she was in high school and her boyfriend L-Rock was murdered in front of her. Spaz' face matched the hooded killer. *All this time I was sleeping with the enemy.*

Spaz stood over her, staring down with the eyes of a madman. He snatched her wallet out of her Coach bag that lay on the counter. He searched through her purse. "I put a lot of money on these cards, 'ho," he said coldheartedly. He pulled out her driver's license and stared at her name that read: Moesha Martini Jenkins. "I should have left your ass in the strip club, bitch." He pulled a blunt from his pocket and took long puffs of the weed and walked toward the door with Grams following behind.

"I am going to miss you, baby." Spaz threw the lit Dutch toward Ronny. Huge flames torched their bodies. Spaz watched as their wriggling bodies began to burn. With no remorse, he headed out the door. Their bodies shook violently from the hot flames tearing through their flesh and bones. The sounds coming from their mouths were never heard by anyone.

Stiletto waited in the getaway car with Slugger in the backseat holding the baby like it was his own.

"This shit ain't right, Slugger," said Stiletto.

"I know. He really losing his mind." Slugger stared down at the baby. "Don't let him hurt this baby, Stiletto," Slugger said, rocking Yasmeen to sleep. "He didn't do shit."

"You think he would?"

Slugger remained silent.

"Oh no, this is foul," she said, feeling guilty.

"Here he comes. Don't let him hurt this baby."

"I won't. I couldn't let him do that." Stiletto felt saddened.

Spaz and Grams walked toward the car while the house burned in flames. They climbed inside.

"Drive this motherfucka!" said Spaz, sitting on the passenger side.

Stiletto's heart skipped a beat, and for the first time in their relationship she felt petrified of Spaz. She drove through the intersection leaving Ronny and Martini's bodies to burn, wondering if Spaz would ever do to her what he had done to Martini.

Chapter Twenty-nine
REMORSEFUL DEMON

No murder had ever bothered Spaz before, but this time he felt bad. Martini was different. He really loved her no matter what problems they had. *Love has a mind of its own,* Spaz continued to tell himself. Even the police questioned him, and with the help of his high-paid attorney, he had no trouble.

Spaz did not want to believe that Yasmeen was not his biological child. He paced back and forth in his bedroom smoking Dutch after Dutch. He finally sat down on the edge of the bed where Stiletto was relaxing.

Stiletto rubbed his shoulders. "What's wrong, baby?"

Spaz took a deep breath. "What if that clown was lying about Yasmeen not being my son and I killed Martini for nothing?"

"She could have got popped just for cheating on you, Spaz. Listen, the only way you are going to find out the truth is to get a blood test."

"You know what? You right. Get dressed, we going to take Yasmeen to the doctor.

Fairmont clinic was a small clinic that Martini had been going to for several years. Spaz never liked going to the doctor. He would simply send her. He knew that as long as she had no diseases then that meant he didn't either. He gave samples of Yasmeen's and his DNA, and after waiting a week, the test results were back. Spaz raced to the clinic by himself to receive the news. Dr. Steinberg entered the room. "How are you, Mr. Henchmen?"

"I am under the weather right now. I need to get the result of the blood test I took last week."

Dr. Steinberg pulled out Spaz's folder and asked him to have a seat. Spaz took a seat with his heart racing. The anticipation was extremely nerve wrecking. Sweat poured from his face as Dr. Steinberg's mouth moved in slow motion. The words were like bullets to the heart.

"The result proved 99% that you are not the father of this child."

Spaz felt like he was on an episode of the *Maury Povich Show*. He rose to his feet and without warning, stormed out of the clinic. Dr. Steinberg watched Spaz race out the doors in disappointment.

Stiletto felt guilty about being the getaway driver when Spaz killed Martini and Ronny. But she had no plans of being disloyal. She was madly in love with Spaz, but also worried about how fixated he seemed to be about Yasmeen. Martini's family would happily take the child if Spaz wasn't the father. Nevertheless, she hoped things turned out in his favor once Spaz left to get the DNA test results. At some point in the day she knew the news couldn't be good when she didn't hear from Spaz all day. Stiletto spent most of the day playing with Yasmeen and watching TV until they both fell asleep.

As Stiletto and Yasmeen lay fast asleep, Spaz entered the house. He walked to the leather sofa and relaxed and rolled up a Swisher filled with hydro. After rolling the weed, he walked to the bar and fixed himself a drink. His vision became blurry after three Swisher's and five shots of Raspberry Absolute. Spaz tiptoed in the bedroom watching Stiletto and Yasmeen sleep. He looked at Yasmeen's face with animosity. Gently, he reached for Yasmeen and carried him into the bathroom. His mind

198

began racing as he ran some bath water until it almost overflowed. The decision was made and now it was time to carry it out. Spaz pushed Yasmeen into the bathtub and began to drown him. Bubbles emerged from his mouth and nose. Yasmeen was losing his life at the hands of the devil.

The bathroom door flew open and Stiletto yelled, "What the hell are you doing?" Stiletto raced to the bathtub, pushed Spaz out of the way, and saved Yasmeen from drowning. He began vomiting water and screaming and hollering.

Spaz snapped. "What the fuck you do that for?"

"Are you out of your fucking mind, Spaz! It's a fucking innocent child! You should be *ashamed* of yourself. You are going to kill an innocent baby? My God!"

"This motherfucker might grow up one day to kill both of us!"

"Is this how you're going to treat our child?"

"What?"

"That's right, you heard me. I'm pregnant."

Spaz grabbed his jacket and barged out the door.

Chapter Thirty
BOSSES OF THE GATEKEEPER

S paz rose to his feet behind a table of gangsters. "I want to continue business with everybody and continue my services of kilos of cocaine for reasonable prices. My supplier, Sticky Scilionni, is now dead. Whatever the case may be, one monkey don't stop no show. The main issue is that it's election time. The mayor is putting police officers on every drug corner in the city. My inside source said it shouldn't last no more than a month. After that, we back in business. Meanwhile, we lay low until this blows over."

One of the bosses from South Philly rose to his feet. "It is none of my business, and I wouldn't give two shits about who we got to kill, but if we got to go to war, then I need to put my soldiers on guard."

Spaz rubbed his beard.

Another young boss rose to his feet. "Yo, we got ya back. I only came to this meeting on the strength of you. We all know that South Philly doesn't like North or West, and we don't like them either."

Pop frowned. "Here you go. We are talking about some serious shit and you bring up our differences."

"You are the reason why my nigga got killed. If they didn't pat me down at the door, I would have blown your motherfucking brains out, pussy!"

Spaz and his men broke up the commotion. "Y'all motherfuckers chill! Now we have to get our shit together. Come on, man. This is unity. I'm speaking about us all uniting as one! If we stick together, we would be unstoppable. There would be nothing that the government, FBI, CIA, or these local mafia motherfuckers could do about it. Look around: we got at least a hundred million-dollars' worth of entrepreneurs in this room. Now, are we drug dealers? Yes, we are! One thing in this life that is guaranteed is death. We can't take this money with us. Nobody can fuck with us! The only people that can bring us down is us!"

Silence took over the room.

Nikki Montagna relaxed in his new office that he inherited from Sticky. He kicked his feet up and puffed on a Cuban cigar. His mood was interrupted by a visitor, who was eager to meet with him. The suit and tie gangster limped into the room with his arm in a cast.

"Hello, Mr. Nikki Montagna. My name is John Polo."

"I know who you are. May I offer you a cigar?"

"No thank you." John took a seat across from Nikki.

"Sticky paid me and my crew to kill Spaz, but the shootout turned bad and Spaz got away. My brother was killed in the process, and Jimmy's body has never been found. I survived the shootout after being left for dead and was lucky to be alive to tell the story. Spaz is a force to be reckoned with, and he has the strongest black army in the city of Philadelphia. He is well known for his brutal murders and genius strategies. He will be your worst nightmare if not handled right. Spaz is responsible for Sticky's death."

Nikki Montagna lost his cool and slammed his fist on the desk and rose to his feet. "We made that motherfucker! I'm not going to let some fucking street punk kill Sticky and get away with it! I don't care if he was Shaka Zulu. I'm going to kill this son of a bitch!" In a rage, Nikki Montagna rose to his feet and pulled a switch blade and kindly slit the guy's neck from ear to ear. "Spaz is a dead man!" he said, holding a bloody knife.

Chapter Thirty-one
LOST SOULS COMBINED

Spaz gave Stiletto a dozen roses. He got on his knees and grabbed her hand. "Stiletto, I love you."

"I love you too, baby."

Spaz cleared his throat and inhaled and exhaled. "Do you remember that day when we were at the Cheese Cake Factory and I told you that true lovers will start off as friends?"

"Yes," said Stiletto.

"I wasn't ready then, but I'm ready now. I want to spend the rest of my life with you." Spaz pulled out a diamond ring. "Will you be my wife, Yolanda?"

"I would love to Spaz but . . ."

"But what?" Spaz said, disappointed.

"You really scaring me with how you've been acting lately. I mean what you did to Yaseem and all. I know we gangsters but damn . . ."

"Look baby, I've been thinking about that. I never prayed in my life, and last night I got on my knees and asked God to forgive me for that. I don't know what came over me. I just want to have a family with you and enjoy my life. Baby, I love you."

"I love you too," said Stiletto.

"So are you going to be my wife?"

She wiped away her tears that rolled down her cheeks. "Yes!"

"I can't believe I'm really getting married. Spaz stood nervously in his three piece suit. The wedding was exquisite. All the members of the Black Boss Family were there to show their respects to Stiletto and Spaz. The temple sat in the middle of Ogontz Avenue and the line to enter was wrapped around. Ballers and players were dressed in their expensive suits, and the ladies were looking extravagant. Spaz wore a white Issey Miyake tuxedo while awaiting his bride and standing nervously beside Reverend Al Smith. Reverend Al Smith was a minister, who some people would mistake for a pimp from the fancy clothes he wore and the luxury cars he drove. His jewels shined from his wrist and neck.

Stiletto was accompanied by her father, Mr. Brown. He walked side by side with his daughter down the aisle. Mr. Brown was a hard-working man who struggled for every dime he had. After his brother died in the war in Vietnam, he started hitting the bottle.

When Stiletto told her parents about the wedding, Mr. Brown became furious. He hated the fact that his only daughter was marrying one of the biggest drug dealers in the city. He held his daughter's arm with a tight grip as they walked up the aisle toward Spaz and Reverend Al Smith. Unlike Mr. Brown, Stiletto's mother was very proud of her daughter for giving her such a healthy granddaughter. She didn't judge Spaz because coming from down south and moving to Philadelphia, she learned that life is what you make it and everybody deserved a second chance. She persuaded Mr. Brown to attend the wedding.

Stiletto would have been heartbroken if her parents did not attend her wedding. Stiletto and her father finally made it up front. Spaz was feeling happy but nervous. He couldn't believe he was finally getting married.

Reverend Al cleared his throat as everyone listened closely. "Thank you, everyone, for attending this beautiful event that only God could allow to happen. Make sure you all come back for Sunday service and don't forget to bring your wallets. We will take money that jingles, but we'd rather have the kind that folds and tingles."

Grams shook his head in disagreement. "Look at this motherfucker—he's a bigger hustler than us."

Reverend Al wiped his forehead with his handkerchief and began to speak. "We are gathered here today in holy matrimony to join together this beautiful couple. Love has again struck and came to conquer these two beautiful individual souls. Is there anyone here that doesn't wish for this happy couple to get married? Please speak now or forever hold your peace."

Every one began looking around for anyone who would not wish happiness on Giovanni Henchmen and Yolanda Brown. If looks could kill, Spaz would be dead right now from the way Mr. Brown glared at him.

Reverend Al took a deep breath. "Okay, moving along. Giovanni, will you take Yolanda Brown to be your lawfully wedded wife through sickness and health till death do you part?"

Spaz smiled. "I do."

"Yolonda, do you take Spaz as your lawfully wedded husband?"

Stiletto couldn't hold back the tears as she replied, "Yes, I do."

Spaz stared in Stiletto's eyes and slipped the ring on her finger. Tears burst out of Stiletto's eyes as she felt the ring slide on her finger.

Reverend Al smiled at the two love birds. "I now pronounce you husband and wife. You may kiss the bride!"

Spaz caressed Stiletto's soft cheek with his hand and moved his face in for a kiss. The two kissed deeply. Stiletto closed her eyes and soared to another world. She thought about her childhood and she thought of the first time she and Spaz met. She thought of all the love she had for him. To her it seemed like the kiss lasted forever, and she didn't want to let go. Everyone watched as they romantically French kissed.

Stiletto had her eyes closed visualizing heaven. She envisioned fireworks in the sky. She could actually hear the explosions. At first she thought the sounds were in her mind. But once she heard loud screams, her eyes quickly opened. What she saw was the Scilionni family holding machine guns in their hands. She thought, *How did they get past security*? But her thoughts were stopped by a hollow-point slug to the forehead. Her body fell slowly to the ground.

The shots took everyone by surprise. Bullets came whizzing past Spaz's face, damn near ripping his head off. He dropped to the ground and took shelter behind Stiletto's dead body.

"Baby, you okay?" he cried, knowing the answer to his own question. She was far from okay.

A shoot-out emerged inside of the church. Screams and cries for help echoed as more shots came from machine guns. Grams pulled his Desert Eagle out and took cover behind the cherry wood seats inside the holy temple. Four shots hit an innocent bystander, tearing huge holes in his chest.

Slugger shot his Glock .40, sending bullets back at the Scilionni family. "Fuck y'all!" he screamed as bullets flew through one of the Italian gangster's midsection, slamming him to the ground.

Spaz noticed the Italian gangster lying bloody and motionless on the floor. Lying next to him was a gun. Spaz crawled toward it while ducking gunshots.

His temper got the best of him. He reached for the gun and went mad, firing shots back with tears racing down his cheek.

Frankie Moran of the Scilionni family was paid by Nikki Montagna to do the hit with a few other men. It was his bullet that struck Stiletto. Spaz fired sixteen shots in his direction. Frankie Moran tried taking cover until a bullet ripped a huge hole in the side of his neck. Blood squirted in each direction. He hit the ground so hard he bounced a couple of times until his body came to a complete stop.

Grams aimed his gun at another member of the Scilionni family, sending bullets whistling past his head. He ducked and began to reload. Grams thought fast and followed his instincts. He ran fast toward the enemy and managed to pump slugs into his body while trying to reload. "Hey, spaghetti head!" Grams shot a hole in his head and watched as his brains wiggled on the ground.

The Scilionni family watched bodies drop from accurate fire from their weapons. Bullets flew in their direction as they retreated and ran for the exits.

When the smoke cleared, people looked around for more danger. Blood covered the floor as mothers and children cried from the horror. Slugger's weapon was empty from firing the clip out. Grams yelled to Spaz, "Yo, let's get the fuck out of here!"

Stiletto lay on the ground in a puddle of blood. Spaz dropped to his knees. "Baby, are you all right?" Spaz got no answer as he watched Stiletto gasp for air. Tears and blood streamed down his face.

"Somebody call a fucking ambulance!" Pain filled Spaz's heart. He couldn't believe this was happening. He screamed.

Mr. and Mrs. Brown rushed over to Stiletto and were hysterical.

"No! No! Not my baby," cried Mrs. Brown.

Mr. Brown showed expressions of grief. "Please God, don't do this to me. Please don't let her die."

Grams tapped Spaz on the shoulder. "Yo, we gotta go!"

Chapter Thirty-three
DISCONNECTED LOVE

Stiletto's funeral was packed with hundreds of friends and family. Five police cars were parked in front of St. John Baptist Church. Stiletto's family and friends were crying and wailing over her death. She lay in the casket wearing a white Gucci dress and white Marc Jacob pumps. Her final viewing was exactly the same as she always was, beautiful and fly. It seemed as if the sun that shined from the window glowed directly off her body and Stevie Wonder's 70s hit, "Ribbon in the Sky," softly played in the background. This was a sad day for all that were acquainted with Stiletto. Sadness spread throughout the church.

Stiletto's arms were folded over her chest as she lay in her cozy, soft, white coffin. The long line of family and friends viewed her body one by one.

Grams and Slugger sat in the back waiting for Spaz to arrive. "Yo, man, I know Spaz will show up for his wife's funeral."

"I hope so. I haven't seen or heard from him in a week."

"I hope he is all right because I need some more bricks."

Grams didn't want to hear what Slugger was saying. "Bricks? That's all you can think about at a time like this, nigga? You're a selfish motherfucker!"

"Why you keep cursing in church, nigga? I'm saying, man, I got to get this bread."

"Oh shit, there's my man right there!" said Grams.

Spaz walked inside the church in an all-black Armani linen suit, black Gucci shoes, and black Cartier shades. His face was covered with tears. He couldn't hide them. It seemed as if everyone grew silent when he arrived and placed their attention on Spaz. He walked slowly to his wife's coffin.

He looked down at Stiletto, feeling guilt and sorrow. He placed a dozen of her favorite red roses in her casket. Then he pulled out a diamond bracelet with BBF engraved on it. As his tears started rolling faster down his cheeks, he put the bracelet on her wrist. "I love you, baby. I will never forget you." He closed his eyes tightly and flashed back to him and Stiletto dinning at the finest restaurants. The first time they made love, their first kiss, and the day they met. His eyes became bloodshot red as he walked away and headed out the door.

Grams and Slugger followed Spaz to his car.

Slugger yelled, "Spaz, wait a minute!"

Spaz turned to see the only friends he had left. "Yo, it's over. I'm out the game!"

"Spaz, you can't give it up now. We came too far." Slugger responded.

Their conversation was cut short by Stiletto's father. "So, Mr. Spaz, are you happy now? Stiletto was the only daughter I had, and now because of you she's gone!" Mr. Brown swung a fast, hard, right punch, but Spaz's reflexes were too quick. He dipped back, avoiding the contact.

Grams quickly grabbed Stiletto's father in a headlock.

Spaz yelled, "Don't hurt him, Grams. Mr. Brown, I loved Stiletto with all my heart. She was all I had. I'm sorry about what happened, but I'm hurting too." Spaz got in his Ferrari and pulled off into traffic.

Grams and Slugger jumped in their SUV and followed.

Mr. Brown stood there out of breath and holding his neck and breaking down in tears at the loss of his only daughter.

The next day Spaz held his baby in his arms. "Look at my beautiful little girl looking just like her mom." And she was a precious sight to see. Light green eyes, honey skin complexion, round face, thin cheeks, and curly hair.

From that day on, Spaz's days became dark. He began thinking about Stiletto and felt a sharp pain in his stomach as he laid low in his mansion that he once shared with Stiletto. As he walked through each room in the huge home, he felt lonely every step of the way. He walked into his daughter's room and smiled at her baby crib. Across from her crib was Yaseem's bed. He could never tell anyone that Yasmeen wasn't his son because he still planned to kill him one day.

Spaz walked to the window and could see the view of the city from his balcony. He lit up a Dutch and started to reminisce. The sounds of the 2 Chainz hit, "Turn Up" came blasting through his iPhone. Once he noticed Slugger's number, he accepted.

"Spaz, I need to talk to you. Please, let's meet."

Spaz knew what Slugger wanted. Slugger was always about making a dollar. *I could give him ten bricks, then give Grams ten and after those deals are complete, fly to California and never come back.* After his thoughts marinated, he replied, "A'ight, I'm a meet up with you in an hour."

"That's what I'm talking 'bout," Slugger said, hanging up the phone.

Mark Rizzo and his fellow agents listened from a parked FedEx van. Mark's adrenaline rushed while thinking of putting Spaz behind bars. *For many years he ducked the system, and now it was time for the system to get some payback.* "Bingo!" Agent Rizzo yelled, after listening to Spaz's conversation with Slugger.

Spaz and Slugger met at BBF headquarters. Slugger walked in nervously as he spotted Spaz in the back drinking a fruit punch while surrounded by his paid assassins.

"Yo, what's up?" Slugger said.

"The sky and everything in it. You two come with me and y'all three watch the door," said Spaz.

"We got you," replied one of the goons.

Slugger followed Spaz into the basement and then into his office, along with two of Spaz's goons.

Spaz took a seat behind the desk. "Have a seat, Slugger."

Slugger took his seat and cleared his throat. "Yo, Spaz, I know you want to leave the game alone but I need you. I need these bricks, man. I can't leave the game. What am I gonna do? Be the average Joe? This is my life. Fuck all these muhfuckas, man. We run this shit! I'm sorry for ya loss. I know Stiletto meant a lot to you, but you got to keep breathing, homie. We the Black Boss Family. We the truth! These niggas is fake. I need you man. I need those keys."

Spaz rubbed his chin. "Yeah, I'm going to give you the best product for the best prices. You know how I do. You family, nigga."

Monsta was on the corner supervising the hustlers, making sure the cash was correct and watching for the police. Grams pulled up on the corner as the younger version of him approached the car.

"Yo, Grams, this is only twenty grand. We are going to need some more work soon. It's money out here."

Grams put the bag of money in the glove compartment. "Yo, I'll have that in an hour for you." They shook hands, and then Grams pulled off.

"Yeeerrrrr!" Monsta said, catching Grams' attention.

Grams pumped his brakes. Monsta walked back up to the car.

"Did Slugger get out of jail yet?"

Grams paused for a second. "What are you talking about? Slugger was never in jail."

"Yes, he was. A couple of days ago, I was up in the suburbs at my girl's crib, and I saw the Feds fucking with him. They pulled him over, snatched him out of his car, and found like two bricks and a gun."

"Are you sure it was Slugger?" Grams couldn't believe his ears.

"Come on, man. I know Slugger. He was in that cranberry Impala. He had on all black with some Gucci sneakers. This was three days ago."

Grams finally put the puzzle together as he looked at Monsta. "Don't tell anyone we had this conversation."

"Come on, man. You know I got you."

Grams pulled off, burning rubber.

Chapter Thirty-four
BURNING BRIDGES

Five minutes later, Spaz rose to his feet. "Yo, Slugger, did I ever tell you that you have been like a brother I never had?"

Slugger's guilt started tap dancing on his heart. He couldn't look Spaz in his eyes.

Spaz smiled. "Come with me. I got something for you."

Slugger followed Spaz to a dark room where Spaz' goons guarded the area. Three men guarded the outside of the door and two guarded the inside. Slugger entered the room with his nerves racing.

Spaz hugged Slugger. "You all I got left, man. I'm stressed right now. I feel funny. Like something is going to happen to me. You know Stiletto is dead, man. My baby is gone forever. I can't believe those bastard's killed my wife." Spaz punched the wall, leaving a fist-sized hole. "Son of bitch!"

Slugger's hand trembled.

"I'm going to leave you in charge of the Black Boss Family. Grams is too hotheaded, and he will never last being on top. I made enough money to bow out gracefully," he said, placing kilos of cocaine on the table. "This here is so strong, you can smell that shit through the bag."

Mark Rizzo observed the front door of BBF headquarters. "He got lookouts," he said, calling for backup. "Let's go get this cocksucker," said Agent Mark

Rizzo. He took his gun off safety and hopped out of the van.

"I thought you'd never ask," said Danny Chambers, cocking back a shotgun.

Spaz' three goons patrolled the BBF headquarters with guns strapped to their waist. A FedEx truck pulled up to the BBF headquarters. Rizzo exited the vehicle holding a package and walked straight up to the front door. Unmarked police cars were nearby waiting on Mark Rizzo's signal.

"I got a package for Giovanni Henchmen," said Agent Mark Rizzo, holding a small box with his hand inside clutching his pistol.

"Delivery?" said one of the goons. He noticed the bulging bulletproof vest under Mark Rizzo's jacket, and he glanced at the unmarked cars parked up the street. "Oh shit, police!"

Mark Rizzo drew his weapon. "Freeze! Don't move! Hands in the fucking air where I can see them," he yelled, stopping the goon in his tracks.

Danny came right behind him with his weapon drawn on the other two BBF members. "Don't move or I'll shoot!" he said to one of the goons who was hesitating.

Fuck that! I'm not going back to jail! The thug reached for his gun and shots were fired. Bullets wrestled the gunman to the ground and folded him into a feeble position. The slugs punctured his lungs and stopping him from breathing.

The other two goons held their hands up and dropped to their knees.

"Hold your fire," said Rizzo.

Patrol cars filled with law enforcement came storming in front of BBF headquarters.

"You heard that shit?" asked Spaz.

"Heard what?" Slugger replied.

"Sound like gunshots or something."

"You been smoking on that loud—got you paranoid." Slugger laughed.

"I think I did hear something," said one of the goons.

"Y'all go check that shit out," said Spaz.

"Say no more," the young thug said. The two gunmen headed upstairs and into the living room. Guns were aimed in their faces and officers wrestled them to the ground.

"You even breathe too loud, and I'm going to blow your brains out, you understand?" said Mark Rizzo.

Spaz had kilos of cocaine laid out on the table. "So you know what's up. You can have this shit, dog. I'm done with the game, na' mean?"

Slugger felt awkward. "You got to do what you got to do, bro," said Slugger.

"Nigga, you need to quit while you ahead too. Fuck you gonna do? Hustle until you get killed or locked up. But not me. I'm out of here on the first thing smoking out of town, you dig?"

Spaz' phone started ringing. "This Grams right here. Hold up, Slugger."

"What's good, b'oy?"

"Yo, that nigga Slugger working with them people," said Grams.

"What!" said Spaz, looking at Slugger with disgust.

"I just got the word. He a informant!"

"You sure?"

"Positive, nigga!"

"Oh shit!" Spaz dropped his phone to the ground and put a gun to Slugger's head. "You're a fucking rat?"

Slugger's eyes grew wide.

Spaz stared in Slugger's eyes, trying to read his mind. "If you are a rat, I can be put away for years, Slugger. You know that, right?"

"What you talking 'bout, dog?"

Spaz began searching Slugger for wires. "You telling, nigga!" he said, ripping his shirt from the front. "Aw fuck!" he yelled, seeing the wires connected to Slugger's chest. Spaz ripped them off and threw them on the ground and stomped it until it broke.

"You a dead motherfucker!" Spaz said. His father's words came to his memory when he told Flash that he and his crew were immune to snitchin'. 'I thought the same thing,' Flash had said.

"Freeze! Don't move! Get your hands up!" FBI Agent Mark Rizzo busted into the room with back-up.

Spaz's heart fell to the ground, and Slugger's guilt took jabs at his conscience. Spaz grabbed Slugger and stood behind him with his gun to his head.

"You motherfucka!" he said to his longtime friend.

"Spaz, don't fucking try it. Put the fucking gun down now!" said Agent Rizzo with his gun staring Spaz in the face. Sharp shooters and FBI agents had their weapons aimed at Spaz.

Spaz swallowed his fear. "I should blow his brains out, and you will have no case!"

"You kill him, you go to jail for life," said Rizzo. "Now put the gun down so nobody gets hurt. It's over, Spaz. Don't do this."

"No, it ain't over. If y'all don't let me out of here I'm blowing his brains out!"

"You know that will never happen. I can't let you go, Spaz."

"Well, he's a dead man," said Spaz, pressing the barrel harder to Slugger's temple. "You sell-out motherfucker. All we been through and you turn rat!"

"Spaz, listen, put your weapon down. You're still young. You will be out to see your daughter make it to college. Don't you want to see your daughter again?"

Spaz grew furious. He knew his life was over. "Fuck this!" Spaz pulled the trigger. No bullets exited the barrel. He squeezed again and noticed the safety was on. "Oh shit!"

Slugger elbowed Spaz in the face, and the gun fell out of his hand. Agent Mark Rizzo and his fellow officers wrestled Spaz to the ground.

"Fuck y'all!" Spaz yelled with anger in his voice.

Federal Agent Mark Rizzo smiled at his prize. "Your ass belongs to the federal government now. We have been investigating you and your boys for years. You're being indicted for drug trafficking and the Rico Act. Your ass belongs to me," Rizzo said, handcuffing Spaz and escorting him to the cop car. "I see you didn't learn your lesson from your friend Reel. Now you're going to live with him in prison." Agent Rizzo shoved him into the back of the cop car and slammed the door.

An hour later, Agent Rizzo arrived at the Federal Detention Center. "Here is your new home. I hope you like it."

"Who the fuck do you think you talkin' to? Do you know who the fuck I am, bitch? But I know who you are: some fake-ass detective. Inspector-Gadget-looking motherfucker. You can't hold me. I will be home by the end of the week. I want to talk to my lawyer!"

Agent Rizzo laughed. "Are you hallucinating? Johnny Cochran couldn't get you out of this one. The only way you will get out of this fucking hole you dug for yourself is to tell me where you are getting all this cocaine from, or I am going to put you away forever, you understand me?"

Spaz bit his words as Rizzo stormed off.

He could not believe what just happened. The thought of Slugger betraying him was alarming. *When it rains, motherfuckers get wet!*

Chapter Thirty-five
POISONOUS SNAKES

Thirty days had passed since Spaz was arrested, and already things were quiet on the streets of North Philly. Knowing that he was a marked man, Slugger's pride wouldn't let him leave the city.

"I am not going to participate in a lame-ass police protection program!" Slugger screamed into his phone at Mark Rizzo before hanging up. He flopped on the bed with his head buried into his knees. Tears began to sprinkle down his cheeks. "How could I do this to my best friend?" he asked himself. "It was either him or me. I would have done twenty fucking years!"

Slugger shook his head. He tried to justify his actions, but felt sickened for helping Agent Mark Rizzo trap Spaz. He rose to his feet and walked over to his built-in bar and poured himself a drink. Slugger's head jerked back as he swallowed the double shot of Ciroc, which instantly made him frown at the hot liquor racing down his throat.

"Fuck! What am I going to do now?" Slugger was in desperate need of a friend—someone to talk to. He knew he crossed the line, and no one would show him mercy. He knew every killer from the Black Boss Family would track him down and butcher him like cattle. He reached under his mattress and grabbed his new .357 snub nose and made sure all the bullets were inside. Slugger knew one good blast in the head from the .357 would take his life. He held it to his head and took a deep breath. The big barrel was pressed up against his temple. The trigger budged slightly from hesitation. Slugger finally managed the strength to pull the trigger. This was it. He began to pull the trigger but was interrupted by the ringing of his cell phone. "Shit!" he yelled. He decided to answer.

"Who the hell is this?"

"Oh, now you don't remember me? This is Teesha, Stiletto's cousin.

Visions of Stiletto's death crossed his mind. "Oh yeah, Teesha. My bad. I'm going through a lot of bullshit right now."

"Aw, poor baby. I am sorry to hear that."

"So what's up? Why you calling?"

"Nigga, I been calling you. You're the one not returning calls. I thought you'd be the one to make me wifey, but I guess not."

"My bad. Just got hit with a lot of shit all at once and had to fall back. A lot of things are on my mind right now"

"Would you like to come over for dinner? That might make you feel better."

Slugger's stomach began to growl, thinking of the scrumptious meal. *Damn, I haven't eaten anything in two days.* "Why not? I need a nice home-cooked meal."

"Okay. Well, you can head this way, and I will make sure I throw something on real sexy for you."

Slugger remembered sex episodes with Teesha and started to get an appetite for her as he grinned from ear to ear. "You still over on Fifty-fourth and Parkside?"

"Yeah, boo. You remember, the third house from the corner. I can't wait to serve you desert after dinner, baby."

"Well, you make sure you keep it nice and warm for me. I'm on my way."

"I'll see you when you get here." Slugger hung up the phone holding his crotch, feeling the urge for sexual pleasure. He quickly showered and got dressed. "If this is a setup I'm a kill this bitch!" he said, pulling out his gun. *"Fuck everybody! These muthafuckas want to go to war then let's go!"* He opened his front door and walked toward his car with his gun in hand.

The night was young, and the sky was just beginning to get dark. Slugger eased down in his Mercedes Benz and climbed behind the steering wheel. He checked the rearview for intruders. Then he placed his gun on his lap, started his car up, and enjoyed the smooth sound of the V6 engine. He checked the rearview mirror again. His heart almost jumped out his chest. Slugger thought he was hallucinating. "What the—"

"Too late for that, you rat-ass nigga." Grams shot Slugger in the back of his head two times. The impact of the gunshots exploded Slugger's head all over the windshield and dashboard. He didn't get a chance to scream. His life was taken by the Grams reaper or as Grams liked to be called, The Executioner. Grams shot five more times slaughtering Slugger like cattle. He slid out the backseat of the Benz with a smile on his face and walked away from the scene as if nothing happened.

"Man, I wish this bitch hurry up." Spaz dwelled on the fact that the judge did not grant him bail and called him a menace to society. The sound of high heels coming toward him got him excited. "About time! I hate waiting in these holding cells."

His lawyer's name was Coretta Scott, a well-known, high-paid attorney who had won more cases than any twenty-eight-year-old African American in the country. Ms. Scott was an intelligent, beautiful, brown-skinned woman. She stood about five-foot eight-inches tall. Her demeanor was like that of a model, very confident and mild mannered. Spaz heard the heels getting closer and started to pace the floor. He overheard her conversation with the marshals. "Come on with all the chitchatting," he mumbled. When he heard the keys jingling. The marshal opened the door, and Ms. Scott entered the room wearing a tight navy dress suit that showed off her frame.

"Mr. Henchmen, how have you been? Not too good I take it. Otherwise, you would not be sitting here."

Spaz stared into her eyes. "I'm in a tight jam right now as you can see, but I'm confident you can get me out. I'm willing to pay you any amount of money to put this nightmare behind me."

"Mr. Henchmen, I want to be clear with you. This case is serious and not a simple task for me. The prosecutors and agents on the case want to bury you. They have been building this case for years, and they have enough to put you away for a long time. So the Feds giving you a chance to cooperate may not be a bad idea."

Spaz frowned. "Are you fuckin crazy? I'm not ratting!"

Coretta Scott knew Spaz was a drug dealer, but she didn't dream that he was this heavy in the game. Even she grew intimidated by his reputation. "This is going to be difficult. They are trying to give you life. I'll see if I can talk it down to thirty years."

Spaz snapped. "Thirty years! I'm not trying to do ten years. Are you out your fucking mind?"

Coretta took a deep breath. "I'm sorry to say, but they just have too much evidence. The best thing to do is to fight it in trial. If we lose, we could come back in front of the Supreme Court and have another shot at beating this case."

"Damn! What the fuck I'm going to do now?" said Spaz, showing his indecisiveness.

Chapter Thirty-six
TRAPPED IN BETWEEN
THE TEETH OF THE SHARK

The same day after court, Spaz was escorted back to the federal detention center. His eyes were bloodshot red. He passed by inmates occupied with playing basketball, watching TV, or sitting in the law library gathered in conversations.

Spaz walked inside his cell, room number 126, slammed the door, and threw his legal folder. "I can't believe this shit!" he screamed.

He reminisced on the moment of his arrest. "Man . . . Fuck!" he said, disclosing the veins on his neck. "I can't do thirty years." He wished for a different result.

"That's fucked up, celli. Well, I'm going to let you get some privacy until lock down. Don't let that shit get to you," said Fatzo, who was Spaz' cellmate. He stepped out the cell and closed the door.

Spaz spent the rest of the day in his cell with tons of stress, aggravation, denial, pain, and misery destroying his psychological and physical form. Finally he drifted off to sleep and awoke from loud screams.

"Lock down!" Ms. Moor announced over the loud speaker.

"Damn, three hours passed that fast?" Spaz asked himself, waking up from a deep sleep.

Inmates began scrambling around at the last minute trying to borrow magazines, books, and fill up their cups with ice.

"I said lock down, gentlemen, so why are you still running around?"

Ms. Moor was an attractive, African American woman who looked like a model rather than a correctional officer. She flirted with inmates of her choice, moving from door-to-door locking their cells. "Get your ass in there, boy." She smiled from ear to ear as she reached cell number 126 and noticed Spaz seated on the bed staring at the walls. He was a jailhouse celebrity with a high profile case.

"Keep your head up, boo," she said, putting a temporary smile on Spaz' face.

"Both my heads is up now." Spaz lusted off her figure.

Ms. Moor switched her rump shaker gently from side to side then looked back, noticing Spaz watching out of his window. *Niggaz . . . all the time these dudes are facing and they worried about a piece of pussy. Well, I'll give him something to look at.* She began switching harder making her cakes jiggle.

"I got to get the fuck out of here!" Spaz expressed to his cell mate.

"I know . . . this shit is out of pocket," Fatzo responded.

Fatzo was from the Logan section of North Philly. "Ay yo, you know what's crazy?"

Spaz caught an attitude. "What's crazy?"

"These rat-ass niggas on the block."

"Who you talking about?"

"Skinny ass Rell and them. They be jumping on niggas cases."

"What do you mean?"

"I call them case hoppers."

"Case hoppers?"

"Man, nobody schooled you to this Feds shit? Well, let me be the first to tell you that these niggas a come in here with a thirty year sentence. Next thing you know they start gathering information on other inmates cases and turn witness against them. By the time these rat-ass niggas finish with you, that thirty years they facing turns into a five year bid. Easy!"

"For real?" Spaz asked in amazement.

"Shit is real. Watch tomorrow when we come out, you'll see those niggas hustling for information. They love the new niggas that come through. They act cool with them and before you know it, they will snitch on him because those rats are wearing wires."

Spaz couldn't believe his ears. "Wearing wires? In jail?"

"Yeah, nigga, you ain't know? These niggas is vicious. Don't talk to them about nothing."

"Man, I'm looking at thirty years in this place," he said, feeling depressed.

"Damn, shit is crazy."

"My own right-hand man ratted on me."

"Ya own peoples?"

"Yeah." *But his ass is dead now.*

"Well, whatever he got he deserved that shit, fam." Fatzo nodded.

"These crackers are trying to bury me," Spaz complained.

"Just keep your head up. These niggas be selling murders."

"Fuck is you talking 'bout?"

"These rats will sell you a murder. They will tell you about a murder, and you give the information to your prosecutor and they will take time off your sentence.

Dead serious. I seen a nigga come in looking at life and was out in three years for giving up info. They use that black phone over there to call lawyers, but instead they calling the fucking prosecutors! Next thing you know, they goin' in."

"Man, how you know all this shit?"

"Because sometimes I talk to the rats to get info out of them. They let me know who telling and who not."

The two conversed into the late hours of the night. Spaz picked his brain for all the information he needed.

Chapter Thirty-seven
UNITED STATES VS GIOVANNI HENCHMEN

At five the next morning, Spaz awoke to the tender sound of Ms. Moor's voice.

"Mr. Henchman, you have court," she repeated herself, making sure Spaz was awake.

"I don't get sentenced until next month," Spaz responded.

"You're on the court list, so let's go," she demanded and closed the door.

"Man, these motherfuckas is drawin'."

Fatzo stretched from a couple hours of sleep. "I told you, it's probably them people wanting to holler at you. I bet you it's the agents wanting to get you to cooperate."

"Man, fuck that. I'm not going!"

"They're going to throw you in the hole if you refuse. Just go see what they talking about."

Spaz showered, dressed, ate breakfast, and lined up with the inmates for court.

After the strip search and waiting in a small cell, he entered a large holding cell full of federal inmates.

The US Marshals began handing out sandwiches and cartons of juice while Spaz wondered what was to occur. He didn't have an appetite. He gave his food to the starving prisoners locked inside the cell with him. Spaz's dream was to be back on the streets in his GT Bentley with his wife Stiletto on the passenger side. He cried thinking of her presence but quickly wiped his tears, not wanting to seem weak.

The loud sound of his name startled him. "Mr. Henchman!"

"What up?"

"Let's go," the federal agent said, unlocking the huge cage. Then he began to handcuff and shackle Spaz.

"Damn, man, all this for me?"

"Yeah, never know when one of you guys will try something stupid."

"Where y'all taking me?" Spaz asked, walking with a limp inside of the elevator. His heart raced, staring at the numbers flashing as he arrived at the assigned floor.

A tall federal agent stared down Spaz's throat. "Showtime!"

Spaz grew angry. "I said where y'all taking me!"

Mark Rizzo stood in front of Spaz.

"What the hell you want?"

The marshals escorted Spaz to an empty room. "Answer me goddammit!" he screamed while getting handcuffed to a chair.

"Ouuww! Man, these handcuffs are too tight!" he said loud and deeply. He examined all parts of the office, and his eyes locked on the view of Center City through the huge window view. He imagined himself clutching the agent's handgun and shooting his way to freedom. But shackles and handcuffs made that idea unattainable. "Like I told y'all earlier, I don't go to court until next month." Spaz stared the gatekeeper in the eyes.

Special Agent Rizzo wore a mischievous expression on his face. He sat in a chair across the table from Spaz and placed a folder in front of him. "Spaz, the king of Philly," said Rizzo, organizing his paperwork.

"What the fuck you want?"

"I'm the Grams reaper. I've come to take your soul."

"I'm already dead, muthafucka."

"You not dead yet, but when I'm finished with you, you are going to wish you were."

"What? . . . Fuck out of here."

Agent Rizzo began opening his folders and began placing photos in front of Spaz. "Do you remember him?"

Spaz noticed the face. *That's Chips backstabbing ass!* "Nope, never seen him before."

"Sure you have. It's your old friend Chips. Good ole Chips. You remember him, don't you? I think you know damn well who he is. You killed him!"

"Hell no!"

"Relax, relax," he said, sliding another photo in front of him. "What about this guy?"

Spaz stared at the photo of a dead body filled with bullets lumping his face. *Oh shit, L-Rock? I had to kill him in order to join the BBF.* "I don't know him either."

"You don't know L-Rock?" Rizzo asked sarcastically. "How could you forget the kid you killed to join the Black Boss Family?"

"I never seen that mutherfucka in my life!"

"There's no need to yell," he said, placing another photo in front of Spaz. "Well, what about these guys from the Badlands shootout?"

Spaz glanced at the pictures of a group of dead Puerto Ricans. *Damn, how the fuck they know I did all this shit? I was protecting myself when we had the shoot-out in the Badlands. Bert was trying to kill me for buying five bricks from him with counterfeit money.* "Why the fuck you keep showing me this bullshit!"

"I know you remember the Badland Massacres because you killed them!" Rizzo said, turning red. "I want you to see what your bullets do to people! Take a good look at them all," he said with anger, placing another photo in front of Spaz. "Here are two kids found dead in their cars filled with bullet holes. And right around the corner from your favorite strip club. Slugger told us everything: how they robbed you for your money and jewelry and you guys came back blasting!"

They shouldn't have robbed me. I didn't pull the trigger anyway, so fuck you. "I told you I don't know any of these motherfuckas!" he screamed, rising out of his chair. "I'm a sue y'all!"

The frustrated Marshals pushed him back down. "Save it! There's no proof you're even here. You went to court, remember?" He smiled, placing another photo in front of Spaz. "Here are two more of your victims. They were cutting into your business, so you had Grams and Slugger kill them, didn't you!"

He sat still with no sign of emotion. *Fuck Maine and Storm.* He remembered sending Grams and Slugger to execute them both for selling in front of his dope spots.

He pushed another picture of two dead Italians toward him, one on the ground and the other slumped over the steering wheel of his automobile. *That's them motherfuckas that Sticky sent to follow me from the Cheese Cake Factory!* Spaz was feeling angry thinking about how Stiletto saved his life by shooting his enemy in the midst of Spaz getting shot.

"How about them, you son of a bitch! I'm going to add them to your body count! I know all about it thanks to Slugger."

Spaz remained silent as the agent showed more photos. "Does this ring a bell?"

Spaz focused on the photo in front of him. His heart skipped a beat. *Fuck Sticky! He got my parents murdered!* "Get this fuckin' picture out my face!"

"Why? You don't miss your old mentor, Sticky Scilionni? Your ass is going down for all these murders! I got another one for you," he said, placing a picture of Nikki Montagna riddled with bullets. "You think Stiletto would have wanted you to go out like this? You looking at life. You better start talking. I want Grams!"

"Make that the last time you mention my wife out of your stinking mouth," said Spaz. "Fuck y'all!"

"Don't make this hard. I got one more for you."

"What's wrong, Spaz? You can't taste your own medicine, you cold-blooded animal!"

He felt like a mouse trapped. *Damn! I might get the fucking death penalty! I'm still young. I can't do no jail time. Fuck! I'm not going to be able to sleep in a real fucking bed. No pussy, no parties, no bitches, no money, just hell! I'm a have to be a snitch then because I'm not doing all this time. No, I got to man up! I'm not no fuckin' snitch!*

Rizzo felt a sense of supremacy. He felt victorious, opening a pack of cigarettes. "You need a smoke, Spaz? Let's be honest. Even though Slugger is dead, the information he gave us will survive sentencing. I will enhance your time to life plus fifty years!"

"So I guess you want me to snitch?"

"I knew you would come to your senses." Rizzo smiled. He reached in his pocket and pulled out a box of cigarettes. "You smoke Marlboros?"

"Man, I smoke anything right now. Just light the motherfucker."

Spaz blew the smoke in Rizzo's face. "Thanks for the cigarette, motherfucker. Now take me back to my cell. I'm not snitchin'!"

"Okay, Mr. Big Shot. You're going to do a mandatory minimum of thirty years for the drugs, and when we charge you for these murders, one or more will stick and you will get convicted. That will add on a life sentence plus twenty years! I know you don't want to be no snitch, but do you think they wouldn't snitch on you, Spaz?" asked Mark Rizzo.

Spaz ignored his comment.

"They would give you up in a heartbeat. All we want is Grams. We know he was your trigger man. We need him confessing to these murders, and we won't even charge you with the murders. And that twenty year sentence can be dropped down to maybe five, no more than ten."

"How the fuck am I to get Grams to confess to anything, if he did do it?"

"We will give you this wire and microphone and all you have to do is get him to confess and you're free."

"Yeah right," said Spaz.

"We're not playing. We do it all the time, although it is almost invisible to the public. The use of criminal informants is everywhere in the U.S. justice system."

"You mean to tell me you a let me out this motherfucka, put a wire on me, and take all my time away if I set Grams up?"

"Exactly. You will do five years and be released to a protective custody program in Arizona and who knows, maybe the drugs we took from you we can give them back for a small price if you know what I mean," said Mark Rizzo, exposing his cigarette stained teeth.

Spaz organized his thoughts and took a deep breath. He stared at the handcuffs and shackles on his ankles. "How the fuck will Grams trust me? What am I going to say? I got a get out of jail free card?"

"No, we're going to give you a bail hearing and have the judge to grant you house arrest until the outcome of the case. Meanwhile, you will wear a wire and an ankle bracelet that will track your every move. Then you will give us the information we need."

Spaz made a deal with the devil. "Fuck it then. Let's do it! You set up the hearing and get me home, and I'll give you Grams."

"Yes! We got a deal!" Mark Rizzo cheered.

Chapter Thirty-eight
PUPPET MASTER

The newscaster held a microphone and started to speak. "Twenty-three year old Giovanni Henchmen was released today on house arrest until the outcome of his involvement of ten thousand grams of cocaine sold to an FBI informer. His lawyer had this to say:

The TV flashed to Coretta Scott. "My client is innocent until proven guilty, and I will prove his innocence to the world in trial."

The camera flashed back to the newscaster. "We will keep you updated on the outcome as we move on."

Spaz drove his black Maserati through the streets of North Philly. He was wired for sound under his black Champion sweatshirt. He wore black jeans and a black fitted LA Raider's hat. His black Jordan's pressed the pedal of the luxury automobile. Spaz stared through the rearview at federal agents trailing his every move. He drove under the West Philly tunnel until he arrived at Fifty-sixth and Parkside. He parked in front of the address and exited the vehicle. His thermal underwear fought off the cool breeze. He walked up a few steps and knocked on the door.

Mrs. Brown answered the door and smiled. "Hey, baby," she said.

"Hey, Mrs. Brown. You mind if I come in?"

"No, come on in," she said, stepping to the side to allow Spaz to enter her home.

"Thanks again for taking care of my child. Did you get the money I sent you?"

"Money is not why I took on the responsibility. My husband wouldn't let me keep it. It's still upstairs in my dresser."

"You keep it, Mrs. Brown," said Spaz, glancing at the bad condition of the house.

"You want to see your daughter?" she asked, leading him inside the living room.

Spaz glanced at the colorful sofa that sat up against the wall. Then he looked at the floor model TV set. *I didn't even know they still sold these.*

"Yeah, I would love to," he responded, anticipating his daughter's presence.

Mrs. Brown headed up the stairs as Spaz walked toward the mantelpiece full of pictures. Spaz picked up the picture of Stiletto and kissed it, feeling a warm sensation in his body.

Mrs. Brown returned with Spaz' daughter in her hands. Spaz took a seat. He felt bad for not visiting Yasmeen at his aunt house.

"She was sleep," said Mrs. Brown.

"Oh, okay." Spaz held his daughter in his arms. She was wrapped in a baby blanket and Spaz watched her yawn. Her breath smelled like baby milk. He smiled and kissed her soft cheek. "Hey, little momma." Kymani smiled and started waving her little hands.

"You trying to bite your hands, mama?" He stared down at her and admired her beauty. "Look at you looking just like your mom," he said.

Mrs. Brown overheard those words and thought about Stiletto. Her pictures decorated the mantelpiece. Mrs. Brown broke down in tears.

"I'm sorry, Mrs. Brown."

"It's okay, sweetie. It's okay. My poor baby." She wept uncontrollably. Spaz couldn't help but feel saddened.

Mr. Brown walked through the front door. "What the hell is you doing here?" he asked with anger, holding a bag of groceries.

"Leave the boy alone, Charles," said Mrs. Brown.

"Get the hell out my house, boy!"

"I was just leaving, just wanted to see my daughter," said Spaz. He handed Kymani to Mrs. Brown. "Thanks for letting me see her."

"Ain't you supposed to be locked up?" said Mr. Brown, moving to the side, allowing Spaz to exit his house.

"I'm sorry to bother you, sir." Spaz kissed his daughter once more and headed out the door.

"I told you don't let that devil in my house," he said to Mrs. Brown.

Spaz sat in his Maserati and got comfortable behind the steering-wheel. He took a deep breath and thought about his daughter and felt mad that he couldn't be around to see her first baby steps and hear her first words. A tear dropped from his eye. His phone started ringing. "What?"

"In no way whatsoever are you to get wise on us, Spaz," said Agent Mark Rizzo.

"Man, I'm not going nowhere. I just wanted to see my daughter. What y'all think? I'm a run?"

"If you do we gone be on your ass like white on rice. We're everywhere."

Spaz noticed the unmarked car parked a block away. He reached into his glove compartment and placed his pistol on his lap. Then he reached in his armrest and grabbed a pair of scissors. He reached down to his leg and cut off the ankle bracelet. Spaz held the phone to his ear. "Hey, Rizzo."

"What is it, kid?"

"Suck a dick up until you hiccup!" he said then hung up. Spaz snatched the wires off his chest and threw them all out the window and sped up the block.

The v8 engine roared like a lion as he reached eighty miles per hour.

"He's fleeing the scene! I'm requesting back up on a black Maserati driven by Giovanni Henchmen. Suspect is marked armed and dangerous," said Rizzo, quick on Spaz' trail.

Spaz entered the highway gliding past traffic at 100 miles per hour. He reached the Philadelphia zoo and exited on Girard Avenue. He made a sharp left off the highway and ran through a red light.

Rizzo and his patrol cars weren't too far behind. "Son of a bitch!" Rizzo yelled.

Spaz went full speed ahead as the massive high speed chase grew intense. "Oh shit!" he said, noticing a cop car coming full speed into him. He turned the steering wheel to the left, gliding through the intersection almost crashing into moving traffic. Spaz pressed the gas pedal and took off up Twenty-Ninth Street at 120 miles per hour. He turned his steering wheel to the right and raced up Jefferson Street.

Rizzo was on his trail, but his unmarked car was no match for the Maserati. "We need a road block on

Twenty-fifth and Jefferson. Suspect is armed and dangerous. I repeat, suspect is armed and dangerous!"

Spaz was at the point of no return. He was on a mission of destruction and no one could stop him. "You don't know who you fucking with!" he yelled. He looked ahead and noticed dozens of cop cars parked with their sirens flashing red and blue lights. Officers were posted behind their cars with their weapons on the hood aimed at his Maserati. "Damn!" he screamed, trying to slow his car down before he crashed into the barricade. "Ah fuck!" he yelled and jumped out of the driver's side. "Ugrh!" He hit the ground hard and rolled over a few times and slammed up against a parked car. He held his gun tight in his hand, rose to his feet and stumbled through the alleyway. Dogs barked as Spaz ran past. He lost his balance, almost falling. He touched the concrete with his hand and pushed himself forward and continued running.

Mark Rizzo slammed on his brakes in front of the alleyway. He got out his car and ran after Spaz.

Spaz ran toward the same motel buildings that got him rich. He ran inside the steel doors, pushing crack fiends out of his way. "Move bitch! Move out my way." He ran up the stairway and saw Monsta at the top floor serving the long line of crack fiends.

"Fuck is going on? Wait in line like everybody else," said Monsta, who was Grams young gunner in training to be a boss.

"Do I look like a fiend, motherfucker?" said Spaz.

"Oh shit! My bad, Spaz. I didn't recognize you." *How he get out of jail?*

"Where is Grams?"

"I don't know?"

"I said where the fuck is Grams!" he asked again, putting a gun to Monsta's neck.

"He in apartment 302."

"Don't fucking lie!"

"He is. Apartment 302."

"Get all these drugs outta here. The cops is coming. Get rid of everything!" said Spaz, running up to the third floor.

Monsta called Grams on his cell phone. "Yo Grams, it's a raid! Spaz is on his way to your room," he said, hanging up. "Got free crack for everybody who block the entrance," shouted Monsta.

Crack fiends and lookouts pulled the metal bolt across the front door.

Spaz made it to room 302. He began banging on the door. The loud knocks made the door shake with each pounding. Spaz knocked some more. "Grams, open this motherfucker, yo! I know you in there." He knocked again.

The door slowly opened. Spaz walked in with his gun in hand. He glanced around the room and saw no signs of Grams. Spaz' gun was knocked out his hand and then the front door closed.

Grams tackled Spaz to the ground. "You ratting?"

"Fuck you talking 'bout, nigga," Spaz said, pushing Grams off him. He tried to reach for his gun, but Grams was too strong.

"You tryna set me up, nigga?" asked Grams, swinging punches at Spaz' face.

"No nigga, they tried to get me too," said Spaz, putting Grams in a headlock.

Grams bit Spaz' arm.

"Ahh!"

He punched Spaz in the ribs, and Spaz returned jabs to the face. Spaz and Grams raced to their feet. Spaz kneed Grams in the stomach and pushed him up against the dresser.

Spaz picked up the gun and aimed at Grams. "Chill the fuck out!" he said out of breath. "I'm not snitching."

"How the fuck you come home on that fake ass bail bond, nigga. The Feds ain't giving those out unless you telling!" Grams said, wiping the blood from his mouth.

"Grams, I played them motherfuckers, yo. I just took them on a ride. I just wanted to kiss my daughter for the last time."

"Yeah, whatever."

"You think I'm lying?" Spaz began taking his clothes off.

"Fuck you doing? I ain't with that gay shit."

"I'm not wired. I threw that shit and put Rizzo on a high speed chase. You need to go out the escape route to the roof and on to the next buildings like Reel trained us."

"What about you?"

"Dog, I'm good." Spaz put the gun down and hugged his longtime friend. "They ain't got shit on me, fam'. I just need you to run this shit and make sure I get my lawyer paid. We may lose in trial, but we gone win on the appeal. They tried to pin all these murders on me, dog. Without Slugger they ain't got shit! That's why they need me to flip on you, but you know that's not happening."

"Nigga, you crazy as hell," said Grams, realizing what Spaz did.

"Look, just lay low and keep shit popping."

Hundreds of law enforcement officers were parked in front of the motels on Twenty-fifth and Thompson. Rizzo pulled out his megaphone. "Giovanni Henchmen, come

out with your hands up! We have the place surrounded!"
said Agent Mark Rizzo.

Spaz peeked out the window and saw the bright flashy
police lights decorating hoods of police cars. He hugged
Grams once more. "Look dog, get out of here. I'm going
to turn myself in. Remember what I said. They don't have
nothing on you. They bluffing. Make sure my lawyer paid
and look out for my kids! Here, take this," said Spaz as he
handed Grams his gun. "It's two hundred thousand dollars
at the BBF headquarters in my office in the bottom
drawer. You got to pull the lever out and twist it and
you'll see it."

"You one crazy mutherfucker. I got you, bro. Don't
worry 'bout shit!" said Grams. They shook hands and ran
in separate directions.

Spaz headed out the door into the hallway walking past
scattering fiends. He headed down the stairs. *Damn, it's
over.* He unlocked the bolt on the steel door and walked
outside with his hands up. The cold breeze sent a chill up
his spine.

"Get on your knees and place your hands behind your
head." Spaz followed directions as officers rushed him
and handcuffed him. Rizzo walked over toward Spaz.
"Hey kid. You thought you could get away, didn't you?
You can't hide from us," he said as they escorted Spaz to
the back seat of Rizzo's patrol car.

"Time to go back home, baby." Rizzo laughed.

Grams watched from the rooftop with a black hood
covering his head. He saw his best friend get placed
inside of the cop car. "I'm the new King! And for all
these motherfuckas that don't like it, I'm a make them
niggas bow down."

Enemy Bloodline
READING GROUP QUESTIONS

1. Do you think Spaz should of snitched on Spook?

2. Do you think Spook should continue to run the Black Boss Family?

3. Do you think Slugger should not have snitched?

4. Do you think Spaz's girlfriend Martini should've been honest about Spaz not being the father of Yasmeen?

5. When Spaz's father came home from jail should he have been harder on Spaz about quitting a life of crime?

6. Were you saddened when Stiletto got murdered?

7. Did any of the sex scenes get you exited?

8. Should Spaz get the death penalty?

ENEMY BLOODLINE

CPSIA information can be obtained at www.ICGtesting.com
Printed in the USA
LVOW10s2359051214

417510LV00016B/676/P